REUNION IN
Tuscany

A Novella

ISBN: 978-1-7753465-0-0
Copyright © 2018 by Ann Camden
All Rights Reserved.
http://anncamden.com
Cover art design by Cover Me Darling
Formatting by: A.M. Williams

❀ Created with Vellum

For Ewan & Evelyn

PROLOGUE

They met in a busy Milan thoroughfare and made love the same day. And before she knew it, she was living with him.

"Stay with me, cara," he'd said. "Stay in Milan for the summer so we can get to know each other better."

What could a young besotted American woman who had nothing to return to really do? The naked, almost vulnerable plea in his eyes melted every bone in her body, and she was hooked. So unlike her.

Everything she did back then was atypical—twenty-one and alone when she arrived in Italy, looking for some fun to try and bury the pain. Her plan was to enjoy herself, then go home and start a new life.

Except she made one fatal error. She fell in love.

CHAPTER 1

*P*atricia Abbott moved through Heathrow's midday throngs, suitcase wheels clacking in her wake. The air blistered, like a jalapeño pepper on an unsuspecting tongue. Moisture beaded on her brow, her palm gripping the suitcase handle clammy now. She usually loved airports, but not this one—and certainly not today.

And that was the crux of her reluctance to travel here. It wasn't the heat so much as the memory of him. This was where they'd first met five years ago. It was instantaneous combustion, which led to an affair that devastated her in more ways than one. This place reminded her of him, of the love she once thought they'd shared.

She walked past high-end shops, her gaze settling on handbags she'd never be able to afford, before it wandered again—and the past and present began to collide. Angst pooled in her stomach.

My God, it **can't** *be.* A frenzied laugh pushed at her windpipe. *Nico.* His arrogant stride said it all.

A person couldn't plan something like this. Never. He was *here*. Nico Andrea Parrettini—the one who'd stolen her youthful innocence, leaving stress, remorse, and pain in its wake. She glanced down as her palm briefly massaged her denim-clad thigh.

A pulse pumped in her neck. Her gaze lingered on him. *He hasn't changed.* Charisma. He had buckets of it. And power. Loads of money, too. And he still seemed indifferent to the female gazes following him.

That blasé attitude could be summed up in two words. Gorgeous Italian. He carried every inch of his six-foot-three body with a barely leashed sensual energy.

She shuddered. But Nico was a man hewn from ice. Cold and hard. A ruthless man. An unforgiving bastard. Their bitter breakup proved that.

If the mental anguish of their split was all she had to suffer that night she'd have felt spared. How many times did she wish it? But the fates weren't with her.

Determined to avoid a face-to-face encounter Trisha melded into the crowd, relieved she didn't have to deal with him. He lived in Milan, while she was going to the Tuscan countryside where she'd been hired to stage a gala wine launch.

She'd almost declined, but needed this job. Her

philandering father's old gambling debts were almost history. It outraged her to be responsible for his excesses. He deserted them, and she was left to pay his bills. This job would set her free at last. No man, ever again, would hook her like some helpless fish on a line.

NICO'S FAMILY WAS TOP-OF-MIND AS HE WALKED through Heathrow. It would be wonderful to visit them and spend some time at his Tuscan farmhouse. He liked getting out of Milan even if he didn't live there full-time. In addition to its crazy pace, it didn't hold great memories for him. Though Milan was a wonderful city in many ways, it was also the place where he was cruelly betrayed.

Christo, he still thought of that woman, still wanted to ensure she was okay, and to ask why she'd deceived him. It was madness, but reality nonetheless. And being in this airport at noon, the anniversary of the date and time they'd met, didn't help.

Then, without warning, his narrowed gaze locked on a svelte redhead flitting through the crowd. His breathing hitched in his throat. Trisha? Could this actually be happening, and on this of all days?

Dio, yes. It's her.

She was still gorgeous with her curvy hips, tight bottom and mile-long legs. A complete package.

The urge to unwrap hit him with the power of a force-ten gale.

He closed the distance between them at speed, slid in front of her and before even thinking about it, clamped his hand around her wrist.

As if primed for this, she stiffened and tried to pull free. "Get away from me." The sneer twisting her lips said it all. She loathed him.

Her, the sinner…

"That's not nice," he said. "Not very gracious of you after all this time."

She tried to yank her arm away again.

"I am not letting you go whether you like it or not. We need to talk."

"But *I'm* not interested in you or what you have to say."

"So what do you want to do, Trisha? Run away again?"

"Me? It was you who tossed me out of your life like a piece of yesterday's garbage."

He flinched, but ignored her comment. "Why did you evaporate into thin air that night?"

"I didn't. You cut me loose, threw a twenty-one-year-old young woman to the wolves of Milan."

"I searched but couldn't find you. In my book that means you vanished."

"I got on with my life. Now, leave—me—alone."

He paused, then lifted his hand from her arm.

"Still a fiery hellion, I see." His eyes narrowed. "This isn't over, so we'll meet again soon." He'd see to it.

Trisha didn't respond as she turned her back to him and began to move away into the crowd.

"Ciao, Nico," she tossed over her shoulder. And that was it. She walked away, and didn't look back.

Trisha checked into her hotel, unnerved by that chance meeting. What did Nico mean when he said it wasn't over? Their relationship ended years ago. Full stop.

She smiled at the clerk when he handed her the room card, and then moved along a mirrored corridor toward the elevators. Once inside she propped her weary body against the black wall. *Who would choose such a gloomy color for an elevator?* But it was a perfect complement to her now bleak mood.

The doors began to whoosh shut, only to be pried apart by two hands. Slick, deft, disturbingly familiar hands… Nico's.

Their gazes locked.

With a fluid movement he stepped in beside her—dwarfing her, commanding the space. She gaped at him. He was bigger than she remembered, but the God-given package that made Nico so fascinating hadn't changed. Thick ebony hair, natural bronzed skin, stunning mossy-green eyes, and squared cheek-bones that flexed when he was annoyed, like now.

But under that perfection beat the heart of a merci-less man who was too explosive for any sane woman to go back for seconds. She knew it, and hated the sudden insight that a part of her would always want him. *How perverse was that?*

Very, although she would never again set herself up for that kind of turmoil. He thought she'd cheated on him, leaving no chance to explain. The bottom line? He didn't want her, like her dear old *Dad* hadn't wanted her mother or her—his only child.

She pulled in a shaky breath. "Why did you follow me?"

He pressed the control panel to hold the elevator, locking them away in a still, prison-like cocoon. He leaned one arm over her head and lowered his face until his steady breathing fused with her uneven breaths.

"Because I don't like it when people turn their backs on me and walk away." His jaw tensed. "And I want to talk."

No chance, chum. "Life has moved on." She shrugged. "There's nothing to say."

"Are you married?"

She inched her head back. *Not in this lifetime.*

"No."

"But you were for a time during the last five years."

Since their breakup she'd never let another man control her destiny. "I've never been married."

"Then why change your name to Abbott?"

A shiver slithered along her spine. She frowned. "How—?"

"My security people tracked you from the airport. They informed me that you, our maestro of one-*up*manship, changed her surname."

"How could they know that?"

"I own this hotel and have access to the records."

She gasped. "That's an invasion of my privacy."

"Ah, but it was expedient."

Trisha knew all about his stubborn resolve. He didn't give up when he wanted something. She managed to stem the outrage seething within, and answered him. "Abbott is my mother's maiden name."

"Why *change* it?"

She lifted one shoulder. "Because I was in makeover mode?"

"It was part of your disappearing act, wasn't it? To make me sweat. That was it, right? Payback time."

"Park your ego somewhere else, Nico. I changed it because I despised my father."

"Ah, daddy issues. That's why I couldn't find you."

Trisha glared at the man who'd been her lover for six months, who she lived with and adored without question, until it crashed around her with astounding speed and havoc. His choice.

"If I did have *daddy* issues I wouldn't have talked to

you about them. I learned early on that your idea of a relationship was sex on tap—whenever you wanted it."

His nose flared with the twist of his lips. He obviously thought her comment was distasteful.

"That's not true. It wasn't all we were about. And if I remember correctly you were a willing partner during our sensual interludes."

Her shoulders and back stiffened. "Yes, but the most positive thing I took away after you threw me out was realizing how self-sufficient I could be." She tilted her chin. "You gave me an hour to pack and leave, treated me no better than a bug under your foot, and when I left I was delighted to see the end of you."

"I *am* getting the hint," he said, his fingers rubbing his neck. "What did you expect? If I wasn't enough and you wanted variety you picked a guy who couldn't turn his head the other way. I don't play around."

"Neither do I, but I'm not having that conversation because you wouldn't believe me anyway," she replied. What I will tell you though, is after leaving I didn't want to see your holier-than-thou face ever again."

Nico's eyes widened as his head moved back and forth. "Call me what you wish, but what are you in all of this?"

"The same person I always was. The one you didn't respect. The one who deserved a more understanding and committed man, and that isn't you."

"And have you found that oh-so-perfect specimen?"

"No. I ultimately decided I'd be insane to put myself through more misery."

"Maybe it's just as well because he probably wouldn't tolerate his woman sharing her body with other men."

Life was a bizarre irony. The thought sickened her. Her father's shenanigans had seen to it.

"You really are a bastard and that remark proved it."

"I suppose from where you're standing I am, and while you still excite the pants off me that's where the attraction ends."

"Yes, we've been there, done that, said it all, and blew it. We were as incompatible as it gets."

A slight smile tugged at the corner of his mouth. "We were either on different planets or you have a twin who shared my bed for six months. There were no complaints from either of us there, cara."

"Trust you to think of it in terms of sex."

"*Trust*?" He lowered his head, his breaths fanning her face. "That's quite a word to be spewing from your mouth."

Trisha edged back, as far as the cramped space allowed. She'd been tried and convicted, given no chance to defend herself, and it still hurt—but she wouldn't give him the satisfaction of knowing that.

"I had a lucky escape."

A scowl pinched his mouth. "And *I* had a rude awakening, because before your exodus I thought you were my woman, but you turned out to be a girl who needed more."

She pulled in a deep, silent breath. This was ridiculous. Whatever they had was done, and so was this conversation. "Do you know what, Nico? You should try to move on. You're in a time warp that's making you a bitter man."

He bit out a low curse. "I have moved on, but am now being forced to remember I was suckered by a girl who had the art honed to perfection, and I loathe admitting that. Defeat is not in my nature."

"I didn't ask you to follow me, so you have only yourself to blame." She tried to reach the control panel. "And now I want to get out of here."

"What floor?" he asked.

"You don't know? And here I thought snooping CEOs like you make it their life's mission to invade the privacy of others."

"Answer me, Trisha."

"Fifteen," she muttered, while wondering how a very intelligent man could get it so wrong, and believe only what he saw.

The elevator lurched upward. Stressed silence bit into the cramped space.

Trisha watched the flickering numbers. Her heart raced as the elevator crawled like a tortoise. When the doors finally parted, she tried to make a hasty retreat.

He snaked an arm around her waist. "Not so fast, cara."

She stiffened as the muscled planes of his chest met her back. He gave up his right to touch her years ago. "Get your hand off me, Nic."

He kept his arm anchored at her waist and slid around to look down into her face. "Nic. I love the breathy way you say that. It still sounds so hot."

Like a bystander pondering someone else's life, Trisha watched his head descend. And by the time she reacted it was too late. He used her startled gasp with a shameless lack of inhibition and pulled her against him, tasting her lips with his tongue, lingering on her bottom lip before his minty taste filled her mouth.

She wanted to push him away but her hands didn't agree with the rational dictates of her brain. The heat of his body plastered to hers and his tongue reaching for hers sent her body into a tailspin. She arched into him, gripped the lapels of his tailored Italian suit and hung on, afraid if she let go her knees would collapse.

A low moan escaped her when he dragged her shirt from her jeans, but reality returned when his fingers began to flit around her navel. She jerked away, straightening her clothes. This was insanity.

"Just go away, Nico."

"Why?" he asked, his rough breaths slicing the static air.

"I never repeat past mistakes and that's what we are." She hated herself right now. How could she have let this happen? She pulled in a steadying breath before glancing at him.

He was leaning against the wall now, staring at her, his expression blank. But his eyes spoke for him. Bright green glimmered there which happened when he was aroused, and when he was angry they sparked with gold.

So Trisha did the one sensible thing left to her. She stepped from the elevator and ran, his parting words "Soon, cara," floating in the air behind her.

NICO TRIED TO CALM HIS RAGGED BREATHING AS HE SENT the elevator down. He hated this. He'd just thrown an adolescent temper tantrum. Only that woman could make him lose his cool. He was tough, tackled the harshest opponents in boardrooms around the world —and won. But when she called him Nic in that low husky voice it drove him insane. He'd never allowed anyone to call him that except her, the she-devil who, in six short months, wreaked mayhem on his previously ordered life.

He lay his head back and squelched a cynical laugh. He didn't have astute judgment when it came to his choice of women. She proved to be just like Angelica who he once loved, and who'd also ground his feelings to dust. At least with Trisha he wasn't naïve enough to call it love.

They'd taught him a vital lesson. Trust no woman with the exception of his mother and sister.

Trisha was gorgeous, but deceitful and self-indulgent. Yet this hunger for her still blazed in him, so he would have her one last time. Sate this hateful need and be done with it. And when the seduction happened it would be in a massive bed, hopefully in the middle of nowhere.

Tuscany would be the perfect backdrop. He knew how to track her down now, so getting her into his bed would be his personal goal when this family time was over.

Tuscany. His next stop. The noose began to tighten around his plans as soon as his brother opened his mouth. "Madre will be delighted to have everyone together for the celebrations at the villa".

Luca wasn't impressed when Nico said his Asian expansion was heating up. He wanted to see his family but it was a busy time. His brother never did bow to the fact that Nico owned a multinational conglomerate which required extensive travel.

"Delegate," Luca said. "That's what all of those top executives of yours are for. And if you can't, you tell Madre you won't be there to celebrate with the family, and *you* handle her disappointment before you fly off again".

The noose had almost choked him then. So he worked overtime, got stacks of extra work done from his home office—and he delegated. Now, with the business pressure off somewhat, he was looking forward to spending time with his family. He hadn't managed a visit in the last few months. Too long. They were close, and he missed them.

This was one of those isolated moments when he wondered if he'd been working too much and maybe missing out on something else. His own life.

Trisha stumbled around the corner and leaned against the wall. This lurking storm cloud called Nico could burst at any time.

"Soon, cara", he'd said. What did that mean?

She pulled her body upright. Nothing. She was overreacting to an unforeseen emotional encounter. Seeing him again brought back memories. Their relationship was explosive—full of hot sex, passionate fights, and equally fiery reunions.

"Focus, Trisha," she muttered as she slid the card into her door. "Leave the past where it is." Today was temporary madness—the spontaneous reaction of two people who once had an intense love affair that didn't have a chance to die a slow death.

Tomorrow she would be going back to Italy. To Tuscany. She once vowed she'd never return, but what successful event organizer could give up such a lucrative opportunity? She did hesitate though.

Until her cousin, Rachael, intervened. "That iron will of yours wouldn't let you turn down such a profitable business opportunity if it were anywhere else on the face of the earth. And who are you trying to convince when you say the past can't hurt you anymore? If it can't, then get on the damn plane and go." Rachael always cut to the chase. "All you do is work, you haven't had a date or a vacation for years, and I think that's *all* about past hurts still controlling you".

Exactly five years since she'd had a break. She did work too much and *was* drained lately. It was unlike her, but she wasn't sleeping well, tossing and turning at all hours of the night… Maybe the Tuscan sun was what she needed. And the money? Manna from the heavens.

SHE LANDED UNDER EARLY-EVENING ITALIAN SKIES AND was ferried to her destination in a black limousine sent by Bianchi Wines.

Trisha's first glimpse of the Casa Girasole stunned her. It was like something out of a fairytale. The huge ivory stone mansion had arched windows and curved wrought iron balconies with masses of flowers in varied shades of scarlet, purple and periwinkle. It sat amidst a sea of sunflowers with stunning views of the treed horizon beyond. This was super-rich territory. She wondered what was ahead of her here.

Nico reeled, and came to a halt at the arched ballroom entrance, his narrowed gaze on the woman who'd just disappeared through the terrace doors. *Trisha? Was he hallucinating, or was it because he'd just run into her in London?*

But no, it *was* her, he realized with a jolt of disbelief.

He crossed the room and was leaning against the doorframe before realizing he'd moved—staring at her Bambiesque legs and curvy bottom in pale green jeans, her hair tied in a ponytail with a yellow ribbon.

"Lost, are we, cara?"

He moved. One step, two…

Then he was next to her, his hands spanning her waist before inching lower to her bottom, palms settling there. "I guess I'm safe in assuming if you're in my parents' home you don't have a lover in tow?"

"I wonder how a smart man can be so *stupid*? Now get your hands off me."

"And there I was thinking you were here to see me," he murmured as one arm snaked up to cup her head.

Luca appeared on the terrace and walked towards them. "Ah, I see you have met my brother," he said, stopping beside Trisha and draping an arm around her shoulders, which dislodged Nico's hand.

Nico gaped at him. *She was here with Luca? She was his brother's woman now?*

CHAPTER 2

He had to be living in some kind of alternate reality. His head swirled with an odd wooziness. *What was it? Shock? Envy? Pity for his deluded brother? Or anger?*

Yes, that was it He *was* angry, because she'd destroyed what they had.

And now she was his brother's woman. How could she have let him kiss her, touch her?

He answered Luca's question. "We knew each other in the past. Quite well, in fact, and I was just asking her why she was here." How could he sound so calm?

"Since I invited her I'll answer you." Luca squeezed her shoulder while flashing her a grin. "She's organizing the gala."

"Ah," Nico replied with a thoughtful nod. "So our party girl has become a party planner. How appropriate." Sarcasm was his only defense because he still wanted to ravish her. And what did that make him?

"If you'd been able to see past your libido you might have got to know the real me, might have understood me better."

"Get out of here, Luc," Nico said without removing his gaze from her.

"Nico—" Luca began.

"Luc, get out. Please. I need to talk to Trisha."

Luca turned to her. "Is that okay for a few minutes? I'll wait in the ballroom."

Nico followed him, slamming one of the mullioned doors before returning to her side. "If that self-serving remark meant I didn't try to get to know you, think again. Christo, I am not a magician, and you didn't share too much personal stuff with me, did you? And don't throw that infuriating blank look at me. I want an answer."

"No, I guess not. What was the sense in sharing details of my life? I always figured you'd move on."

He clicked his tongue. "That's rubbish and you know it. You were a closed book from the moment we met."

"I had my reasons."

"And by the sound of that comment you are the same mysterious woman who slept in my bed for six months, the woman I cared for deeply but who I never knew. You prepared gourmet meals and filled me in on every damn aspect of Five Star cuisine..." he closed his eyes, opened them "…and joined your body with mine in the most intimate way a woman and man can share, but I didn't know you."

His voice shook like a leaf in a windstorm. "I don't know if you have any living relatives, where you were born, if you had the mumps or measles, or anything else about your life before we met."

"You never wanted to know the real me. You came, saw, conquered and judged, and *you* were wrong."

"Not true. I wasn't permitted inside that closed head of yours. And judge you? I only had your behavior to go by." He rotated his shoulders in an effort to ease the tightness there. "You liked to party and I was exhausted watching you."

"You worked and read medical textbooks and I was bored stiff."

"I had to work. I thought you understood that, but now I see our relationship was a sham, a lie. You never planned to give us a chance, did you?"

"I wasn't allowed. Cast your mind back, Nico, and remember this. She stabbed the air with her forefinger in unison with her words. "I—was—discarded. Why? Because I couldn't live up to your lofty ideals and impossible standards."

"Forgive me if I appear to be Stone Age man but I need monogamy from my partner."

"Stone Age man got monogamy."

He clenched his hands as he watched her, noted the agitated look on her face, waited…

"I was never your partner, just your temporary diversion," she said. "And I always guessed, deep down, that you were just passing through."

"Why would you think that?"

"You lived in Italy and I lived in America. That was all we needed to know."

"If we had lasted would you have moved to Italy to be with me?"

"Would you have moved to America to be with me?"

"Touché," he murmured. "But not an answer."

"No, I wouldn't have. We didn't have enough going for us."

"Listening to you now makes me wonder if you have our relationship confused with another one." He edged closer, snaked one arm around her waist and cupped her head. When he loosened her ponytail her hair spilled over his hand in silken disarray.

He buried his face there. It was a mistake but he couldn't help himself. She smelled wonderful, like a flowering Lilac on a sunny spring day. Then his brain abandoned him and he moved his head until his mouth touched hers. He flicked his tongue over her lips before pushing through them, reaching for and meshing with hers.

The kiss plundered. He kissed her in anger. He kissed her for revenge. And he kissed her with passion. His arm tightened, clamping her to him as the hot pressure of his tongue continued to dance with hers.

Nico grunted when she wrapped her arms around

his neck. His hand strayed and cupped her breast, toyed with her nipple—and still he kissed her with the wildness of a man who'd found something he didn't know he'd lost.

It ended as suddenly as it began.

Trisha's fist hit his shoulder as she wrenched out of his embrace. "I hate you."

"No, you hate wanting me just as I do you, but if I have to live with the reality that I can't be in the same room as you without wanting to rip every scrap of clothing from your body, so too should you live with your reality. And that, cara, is you *do* want me." Then he walked to the terrace steps and away from her without a backward glance.

"COAST CLEAR NOW?" LUCA ASKED AS HE STROLLED INTO the room several minutes later.

Barely. But she hoped Nico would be gone long enough to get her wits back. The lurking headache she began the day with now strummed a heavy rhythm against her skull. "I wish you'd told me your brother's name."

"So you know Nico." Pokerfaced, he leaned one shoulder against the wall. "But I couldn't have known that, nor that it would be a problem."

No, neither of them could, and now she had to deal with it. Avoiding him would be her best option.

"Why do you and Nico have different last names?"

"I use my mother's maiden name for the business. We are Bianchi wines started by her ancestors, so it makes good sense. And I also wanted to win on my own without Nico's success overshadowing my business decisions."

"I won't deal with him, Luca."

"I hear you but *I* can't control my brother."

And there was the problem. What was Nico going to do? Better yet, how was she going to handle him?

"I would love to know what went down with you and Nico."

"Nothing."

"The word 'nothing'," Luca said, "implies no emotional involvement, and the emotions flying between the two of you are very intense."

"Mutual antipathy," she said.

"And that's a very powerful emotion, is it not?" he asked, watching her intently.

NICO WAS LEANING AGAINST HIS BLACK FERRARI, DOOR ajar, forehead bent on the car's hood, when Luca caught up with him.

"What the hell was that about back there?" Luca asked.

Nico's head shot up. "Are you sleeping with her?" Curt, abrasive words…

"Are you jealous, big brother, and would you believe me if I said no?"

He slammed a fist against the car. "*Luc!*" Dio, but this was a nightmare.

"You have no right to ask that. My sleeping habits are none of your business."

No, he didn't. Not anymore. "She and I—" He wasn't lost for words very often.

"I *did* pick up on that," Luca said.

"And it doesn't bother you?"

"Why should it? It's past, although I think you were crazy to let her get away."

"Here's to you being able to handle her." Nico's voice was laced with doubt as he folded his body into the car's black-leather interior, revved the engine, and without another word sent it down the winding, tree-lined drive.

TRISHA GAZED ABOUT THE BALLROOM FROM HER PERCH on the ladder. What a wonderful place for the celebration. The recessed window alcoves which spanned the vast ballroom's length were perfect for the wine displays and to house the food stations. She looked at the map she'd drawn on her computer. One end of the room would be set up with round tables and stools, the center of the ballroom would be used for dancing and at the head of the room would be the Italian tenor and back-up brass band and violins she'd booked before leaving Manhattan.

"You look busy. Need some help?"

Nico… Who could mistake that husky drawl? She'd found out his home was nearby, on the far end of the Parrettini estate, which meant he'd be around a lot, and she'd have to learn to deal with it. "No, but thank you for asking."

"*So* polite, but you should come down from there. That ladder is skewed a bit."

"And?"

"*And* if you start to fall I'll have to catch you." He chuckled. "You'd finally be back in my arms."

She ignored the ladder's last step, and with one thud landed on the blond-and-russet parquet floor. *Dumb, Trisha.* The jump caused the old, familiar pain from her accident to knife along her thigh.

Then she glanced at him. His jeans fit where they touched and that white T-shirt hugged him in all the right places. She gulped.

He arched one dark eyebrow. "And *hello* to you, too."

Damn her roving gaze. He would have to rub salt in the wound, too, wouldn't he? And speaking of wounds… She rested her leg on one rung while leaning her elbow on another. If she supported her leg it helped to ease the pain. Then she steeled herself to look at him again, and wished she hadn't.

His narrowed eyes were examining her leg. He walked towards her. "How did you hurt yourself?"

His gaze was fixed on the scarring that started on her outer thigh just above her knee, and got lost under the hem of her shorts.

She didn't need this. These were longer shorts but once she lifted her leg they rose with it to showcase the scarring she hated, but had learned to live with. She slanted it away from him. Too little, too late. "I cut it."

"That must have been some cut."

She shrugged. "It was a long time ago."

He stopped in front of her. "How?"

"I fell."

"Some fall, hmm?"

"Yes."

"And are you going to enlighten me?"

"No."

"Why not?"

What was this? The Spanish Inquisition? "It's a scar, for God's sake, and doesn't require an in-depth analysis." She was distraught, careless, back then, and he was the last person she'd talk to about it. He'd kicked her out and she was hit with a car when she ran into the rainy Milan night. It was horrible—the pain, the operations and therapy, being alone in the Rome hospital so far removed from home...

"I think you'll tell me when you're ready."

"No, I won't," she muttered in an undertone meant for her ears only.

"I heard that."

"It's old news, Nico, and I have things to do." Their discussion was over. His scrutiny would intimidate most people but she refused to let it fluster her.

"So I will let it go until you're ready to tell me but—"

The flash of disbelief on his face didn't escape Trisha's notice. Her gaze followed his to the room's open arched doors.

Could it get any worse than this? Gina Rossini. The oh, so suitable Italian woman—beautiful, voluptuous and statuesque. She once gave Trisha her spin on Nico's needs. "Nico will have his fun for a while but he *will* settle down to have babies with an Italian woman who understands his culture." Translate it to mean with Gina.

"*Nico,*" she murmured, sashaying towards him while throwing Trisha a poisonous glare.

Someone poured her into those shorts. Being snide wasn't something she ever stooped to, but she'd never met a more hateful person than Gina.

She pulled a face as she watched Gina press her body against Nico's with cookie-cutter precision, drape her arms around his neck and push her fingers through his hair.

He didn't seem smitten. He frowned and dull red scored his cheekbones as he removed Gina's arms and stepped back.

"Oh, Nicki, don't be a spoilsport."

Nicki? Cute.

He reached for Trisha's hand. "We'll see you later, Gina," he said, turning towards the terrace doors.

Saved from the she wolf. Almost, Trisha thought when she glanced up and noted the sneer contorting Gina's face. Hatred. *And all of it for me.*

"Let go of my hand, Nico." They'd reached a far corner of the tiled terrace. "I have work to do."

"No. Despite our non-relationship there are things I want to know, so think long and hard before I ask you again."

"I don't owe you explanations," she said.

"You think not?"

The rigid clamp of his jaw told its own tale. He was in grim mode, much like the stormy clouds scuttling across the sky. This was shaping up to be a day from hell.

Then Luca showed up, and she inched away from Nico. "Ah, here you are Trisha." When he reached her side Luca wrapped an arm around her waist. "I have to go to the vineyards. Come with me?"

"I think slow water torture would be better than being here," Trisha said.

His probing gaze studied his brother. "Upsetting our guest again?"

Nico winked at her and held her gaze. "We do have a unique flair for bringing out the worst in each other, don't we, bella?"

Luca let that pass. "Will you be joining us for

dinner?"

"Of course," Nico said. "I wouldn't miss that for the world."

"Then we'll see you there and hope you can manage it without distressing Trisha."

SHE TRIED TO BEG OFF DINNER WITHOUT SUCCESS. THE family expected her to join them, so she had no other choice—and adapting to the stress of it all would be essential. She was still trying to determine how to handle it as she approached the main salon just before eight that evening. One hand fiddled with the stray tendrils escaping her chignon, the other smoothed away the non-existent wrinkles in her navy-blue silk dress. The pain in her hip was unrelenting. She had jumped up and down the ladder too much, but it was necessary. There were four days to get through, and each one was shaping up to be a trial.

And how. Her heart quickened as she opened the heavy salon doors and stepped inside.

Nico was the first person she saw, and he wasn't alone. He stood to one side with a baby strapped to his chest, his arm wrapped around a beautiful raven-haired woman. Was he married? Was the child his?

That possibility bothered her when she knew it shouldn't. His life was in Italy, so why expect anything else? More to the point, why was she upset? Because once, when she was young and in love, she became a mere convenience to this man—and the gullibility of her twenty-one-year-old-self stunned her. But she was wiser now… Wasn't she?

Then she surrendered to a healthy dose of anger.

This was the one who'd been all over her like an ant at a picnic, not once, but twice. The one who'd, five years ago, spat his venom at her and called her every vile name in existence because he believed she had an affair. She didn't.

Her gaze collided with his watchful one. He might be scared she'd talk, tell all to this woman, but she would never hurt an innocent person to revenge him. He must at least know that about her. Thanks to her father's malice and affairs with so many women, she was the innocent enough times in her young life to understand how it felt. It had embarrassed her so much… They'd lived in a small town and her father didn't hold back. Everyone knew what a philanderer he was. He even came to her school and flirted with a few of the girls there until one dated him. She clenched her hands into rigid fists.

Luca's voice dragged her back from her painful past. "I was just about to come looking for you, Trisha." He smiled and strode towards her.

"I was enjoying the view from my balcony and time got away from me," she said. Not true.

"Good. We all need some down time. Now come, I'll introduce you." He anchored his arm at her waist just as the woman slid from beneath Nico's arm and strolled forward, both arms extended toward them.

Misery swamped Trisha. *What could she say to this beautiful woman?*

Then the woman was squeezing Trisha's hands. "Luca has told me much about you, Patricia. I'm delighted we meet at last. I am Isabella Carlucci, long-suffering sister to these rogue males." She tipped her head towards her brothers.

Sister? Nico had never talked about his family, which said a lot now. They were obviously close, but with the exception of an accidental meeting and subsequent dinner she and Nico had with his mother in Milan, she was never privy to that part of his life. Temporary diversions like her were never taken home to mother.

When she glanced at him his reaction floored her. He winked, a slow, flirtatious flash of one green eye.

He knew she thought Isabella was his wife. Worse still, her body language had given her away, and showed him it bothered her. He always was an ace at reading her. But did he ever really know her? No. Did he try to? No.

He said he did but thought she cheated on him, which quashed that one. He was astute, brilliant and successful, *super intuitive*, but still believed she had other lovers.

"Patricia, my dear, it is good to see you again. You look wonderful."

Trisha pushed her reflections aside and smiled as his mother approached her with open arms.

"And you," she replied as Annalia kissed her cheeks. "I had no idea it was your home I would be visiting and working in."

"No, I am *quite* sure you didn't," Annalia responded with a wry twist of her lips.

Isabella's startled gaze moved between them. "You know Patricia?"

"Si, we met briefly five years ago in Milan."

"Ah, Milan," Isabella echoed with a knowing shake of her head. "I see." Her gaze darted to Nico, then to Luca's hand resting at Trisha's waist.

"And look, here is Marco," Annalia said, turning as the doors opened again.

His father was what she'd imagined Nico would look like in twenty-five years.

Trisha watched the tall, greying man approach her. Then, to her surprise, he bestowed a kiss to her cheeks.

"Our father," Luca laughed, "and Alexio, Isabella's husband," he said of the man who'd followed Nico's father into the room and was shaking her hand.

NICO COULDN'T BELIEVE IT. HIS FAMILY SURROUNDED Trisha like a defensive moat, which kept him from getting too close. She drew people like a magnet. Always had. And now his family was under her spell.

What was he going to do about that? What could he do?

She was Luca's woman, his family her personal fan club. How would he handle Trisha as a part of his family, but not a part of his life? She would be at family events with Luca. Would they get married eventually, have children? He'd have to find a way to accept and move on.

He strolled towards them. "Well this is nice, a *love fest.*" *It didn't look like moving on would be easy.*

Annalia glared at him while his father slapped Nico's shoulder. "She's a delightful young woman. Where was your head when you let her get away?"

Could silence speak? Nico glanced at Trisha whose face was bright pink now. His father's comment embarrassed her, but she probably didn't like being reminded of what she saw as the biggest mistake of her life.

Isabella broke the strained silence. "Nico, I'll take the baby and settle him before we're ready to eat."

"There are name cards at each place," Annalia said as they entered the dining room, "and yes, Nico, we have spaghetti and meatballs for you. And, of course, I've included our crispy cheese pizza for Patricia. Do you still like pizza?"

"Always and forever," Trisha replied.

"How strange," Nico murmured. "I didn't know you *did* forever."

"Yes, if I'm with someone who also *does* forever."

"Bravo, Trisha." Luca grinned as he slapped his

hands together with several sluggish cracks.

Annalia's withering glare would have silenced weaker men, but not her sons.

Nico chuckled as he conceded defeat to Trisha with a formal bow from the waist.

Then their attention went to the table. Luca pointed out her name card before she located it herself It was next to Nico's.

She cursed the fates that seated her there, and even worse had him pulling out the chair, his fingers lingering at her neck.

The brush of his fingertips caused needle-sharp shivers to prickle there. Why was he trying to unnerve her? Who could figure him out? He had no right to touch her. Not anymore. But how could she stop responding?

Trisha tried to ignore him, except every time he moved his leg pressed against hers, and if she pulled away, he followed with a subtle pressure. There wasn't much between her silk dress, his lightweight black evening wear, and hot skin.

While he talked to his father, he moved his hand down until it rested on her upper thigh.

His fingers curved inwards, flexed, straightened, flexed again.

Oh, my God. What is he trying to do? Prove I'm not immune to him?

No, that he was immune to her, more like.

Two could play this game.

Her fingers moved to return the favor but just as she applied pressure, he placed his hand on top of hers. It only took one glance to notice the bright green sparking in his eyes.

Trisha tried to pull her hand away but his grip tightened. For several minutes they sat like that—mute, her hand gripped against his thigh, neither of them eating. How could they eat with one hand? When Annalia inquired about their appetites he released her hand, and they concentrated on their food.

Amid the animated conversation they talked about restoring old properties—he about his farmhouse, she, the Maine cottage left to her by the great-aunt she'd met as a child. Nico also talked about the pressure cooker his business had become during the past year.

"You and Trisha seem to have a lot to talk about, don't you?" Luca said.

"We're seated next to each other. It's natural that we talk." He leaned back, folding his arms at his chest. "Trisha and I are trying to catch up, that's all."

"I'm sure you are but I think I'll steal her away to show her our evening sky. It's stunning and shouldn't be missed," Luca said.

Annalia rose from the table, her knuckles white where they gripped the grape-back mahogany chair. When she spoke her smile was serene. "Forgive me, but I must check on dessert." Her narrowed gaze targeted Luca. "Could you help me in the kitchen for a moment?"

"WHAT ARE YOU TRYING TO DO?" SHE DEMANDED AFTER clicking the kitchen door shut. "Start a war?" She rolled her eyes. "God grant me the patience to handle my adult children's intrigues."

Her gaze drilled into Luca's. "You better know what you're doing," she said. "And get it over with soon, because I can't stand this conflict within my family."

"Trust me, Madre. Twenty-four hours and things will be okay."

"Trust? You listen to me, Luca. Nico is your brother, and he might never have said it or even admitted it to himself, but he loved Trisha. I don't know what happened but neither do I want to see him hurt again, so you tread carefully here."

Isabella slammed through the door and was beside Luca in a blink. "What do you think you're doing?" she demanded, fisting her hand and thumping his arm. "You should not be with her. It will make Nico uncomfortable."

Annalia sighed. "That was several years ago, and life does move on."

"Madre is right," Luca said. "If he couldn't hold on to her that's his problem."

"Well I think it's low, insensitive."

"Do you know, Bella, I don't care—"

"*Stop* it, both of you," Annalia cut in. "I won't tolerate a rift within my family."

CHAPTER 3

After coffee and dessert, Nico had a hazy recollection of his family's mass exodus—Luca to a business appointment he told Trisha he couldn't miss, Isabella and Alexio to their home, Marco to his library, and his mother to do whatever mothers did in a villa that sported twenty en-suite bedrooms and countless other rooms.

With the final click of the door it was just he and Trisha, and the sensual buzz still raging in him. He shifted in his chair. Sitting beside her during the long, formal dinner had been torture.

She was a stunning woman but... He leaned close and whispered in her ear. "Now that we're alone—" He cupped her head with his palm like he used to. "—I can get rid of this." His other hand began to pull the pins from her hair.

"Stop, Nico, it keeps my hair out of my face," she

said while trying to squirm away. But his palm kept her anchored there.

"Tough. We both know you aren't reserved. You're a firecracker, not a prude." And with that he pulled out the remaining hairpins.

Gleaming waves fell loose to graze her shoulders.

"And when did you start wearing dreary colors, dresses that cover you from your chin to below the knees?"

"I'm not a twenty-one-year-old girl on vacation. I'm here on business."

"That's a copout and you know it. My grandmother showed more skin than that when she went to church on Sunday. Dio, what happened to the woman-power beliefs you showcased on that Minnie Mouse T-shirt you once lived in?"

WHAT INDEED? SHE'D RUN OFF TO ITALY TO ESCAPE THE smothering grief she felt after her mother's death. Yet, despite her sorrow, she still loved life, thought anything was possible. And that T-shirt proved it—a smiling Minnie Mouse with both hands fisted above her head, 'Girl Power' captioned above in bright green and purple.

Her mother made Trisha a strong person, reminded her constantly she was smart and valuable, and could do anything she chose with her life—always reiterating the fact her father was an anomaly who had nothing to do with them. Still, he'd humiliated her many times during her young years.

But when Trisha saw that T-shirt it seemed a perfect tribute to her late mother's guidance, as well as her own future. She'd bought three of them.

Then she met Nico, and learned more about life's harsh realities than she'd have thought possible.

She ran away five years ago and had, she realized now, been running ever since. Running from ghosts. Her past was littered with them. Running from the revolting memories of her father, her bitter break-up with Nico, and from the pain and isolation of her accident—running, running, running…

"Minnie Mouse and Girl Power got lost in life's struggles." And she would be wise to remember how dreadful it had all been. With the exception of her cousins, everyone she ever loved disappeared in one way or another. But the way he'd treated her did her in.

"We all have to grow up eventually, don't we?" she said in explanation. And with that comment, she moved away from the table and towards the salon door.

THE NEXT DAY NICO STAYED AWAY FROM THE VILLA. HE wanted to see Trisha, but after she'd walked away last night he knew she needed space. So did he. She definitely had more going on than just father issues. *What happened in her life?*

And now, while strolling onto the terrace in the evening he noted she had her hair in that priggish bun again. *Defiant little witch.* He smothered an appreciative smile. Her mouth was sealed in a tight stubborn line, her chin was up and her eyes, icy blue orbs now, said she was ready to take him on. More like the old Trisha. Ready to fight her corner.

But the hair would have to go.

He sat beside her and freed it with a flick of his wrist that sent the hairpins flying.

Trisha let out a startled gasp.

"Ah, much better." He pushed his fingers through it until it cascaded around her face in a flaming mass.

"I agree with Nico," his father said. "Your hair is much too lovely to hide."

"Leave it alone, Marco," Annalia said. "It is, after all, *her* hair, and others might also try to remember that?"

"Ciao, everyone. Sorry I'm late," Luca said as he joined them.

Nico stiffened as he watched Trisha. Just the sound of Luca's voice and she smiled. Dio, he tried to rationalize her response but still hated it. Then his gaze moved to the tall, blond woman holding Luca's hand.

What was this?

"I've brought someone I want you all to meet." Luca smiled at the woman next to him. "This is Jan Berkston from California, and as most of you know, we've been dating for several months now. Jan, you know Trish—"

The rest of Luca's words were lost on Nico as his glass clattered down to meet the table's glass surface. *Luca had another girlfriend? And Trisha knew her? Was this a new-age spin on kinky or something?*

"And this is my brother, Nico."

He stood, weathered the introductions without losing his cool, and waited for Jan to be seated. Then he moved. He bent over and shifted with fluid ease to pull Trisha's chair back.

"It's time Trisha and I talked." But she didn't move.

"I could lift you out of there very easily, cara," he said in steely warning when he noted her hands clamped to the chair.

"Excuse us," he said to the hushed group. He grasped her wrist and pulled her behind him, moving away from the terrace. Luca's soft laugh and a quelling shush from his mother followed them.

"That was rude and embarrassing," she said as he marched her to his car, pressed her inside and secured her seatbelt before striding around to fold his body into the seat beside her.

"Nico."

"*What?*" he said as with one fingertip flick the car roared to life, and he gripped the chunky gearstick to send it careening down the drive.

"Where are we going?"

"To a place where we can talk."

"There's nothing to say. You said it all five years ago, remember? 'Get out, I never want to see your lying, cheating face ever again'. I wanted you to listen to me then but all I saw was your back as you spit out those same pig-headed words. *'Get out'.* So I did, and never looked back."

"I'm sorry I didn't listen. I have a volatile temper at times."

"Not good enough. You called me a tramp and a sl—"

"I was very angry with you," he cut in. "But when I calmed down I *was* worried, had no idea where you were, if you were safe…"

"I survived without your concern."

"Christo, I thought you had died and no matter what my sins were it was unfair of you to do that to me."

"Do that to *you*? How could I have guessed after the way you exiled me? And after leaving your apartment *I* was more worried about having enough money to get from Italy to America than your finer feelings."

"Why didn't you use the credit cards I gave you? What did you think they were for? To add sparkle to your wallet?"

"And using them would have made me what? A kept woman? What a repulsive thought. I never used those things the whole time we were together, and every one of the meals I cooked was made with my money." She pushed her forefinger into his upper arm. "*Mine.* I might have lived with you but didn't want your money, so you can be sure the only way I'd get home would be by the sweat of my brow if necessary, but never, ever, with your money."

The car bounced into a field and ground to a halt. He thumped the steering wheel. "I don't care about dollars and cents, do you hear me? I'm saying I was worried about you, and you're jabbering on about money for *gourmet meals?*"

"You must have had a guilty conscience."

"Yes, dammit, I did. Does knowing that make you feel better?"

She glanced at him while reaching for the door handle. "No, it doesn't."

Nico foiled her escape with one tap to the remote locking mechanism and switched the interior light on. "You are not in the Big Apple where cabs can ferry you about. How did you meet Luc?"

Her gaze met his. "I've never seen anyone who can change the subject with such slick ease."

It's one of my gifts to mankind," he said, resting his head against the leather headrest. "So, how did you meet him?"

"I don't see why—"

"Humor me," he interrupted.

"An international wine fair in California. I was at the opening reception."

"And after one short meeting Luc decided you were

the ticket? The only one who could pull this gala off in style, was that it?"

"Not exactly."

He lifted his head and stared at her. "What *exactly* then?"

"I invited him to several events so he could see my work first-hand."

"And you became friends, si?"

She smiled. "We did."

"And that was it?"

"No, I slept with him so I could secure a very lucrative contract for my business."

He didn't believe her. "Don't talk like that. It's not becoming."

"But there's nothing becoming about tramps, is there?"

"Enough. You are no tramp, just a mulish woman determined not to give me half a chance here."

His chest heaved as he sucked in a deep breath. "Christo, I thought you were his woman. Did you know that?"

She grinned.

"I don't find it amusing."

The grin morphed to a warbling laugh. "It really is, Nico. I mean, *Luca* and me? Where would you ever get such a ludicrous idea?"

Where indeed? And he would be chatting with little brother who'd managed to plant that seed so securely in his psyche. Was it a calculated act, or a fortuitous one? Definitely intentional, he decided. *But why? What was Luc's agenda?*

"You have to admit, Trisha, the two of you appear to get along well."

"Yes, we do, but despite your twisted mind I don't jump into bed with every man I meet, and I do have wonderful male friends."

"I am not twisted and you get along *very* well."

"If you believe intimacy and friendship go hand in hand what do you suppose our biggest problem was?" she asked.

"You see, this is what you do," he said in a rasping voice. "You use that temper to stab me with your cheap shots and beg off with a return jab when I call you on it." He drummed his fingers against the cherry-wood dashboard. "And that's one of the reasons we always ended up in a battle."

"Spoken by the man who just owned up to his own volatility and who always stabbed me back, usually with a cheaper shot."

He grinned. "We are both hot tempered and stubborn. Neither of us wanted to give an inch, did we?"

"And even if I did try to talk you couldn't deal and resorted to your other cheap-hussy solution—you dragged me off to bed, or *not*, for a bout of sex."

"You were no hussy nor did we just have sex, although even I was challenged by the discomforts of a bricked terrace," he murmured. "But sometimes our control deserted us."

"I'm not having this discussion."

"Not too young and not at all stupid," he said while reaching over to unclip her seatbelt.

SHE TENSED WHEN HIS TONGUE TEASED THE SPOT BELOW her ear. He smelled familiar, fresh and spicy, like a forested glade after a new rain.

It felt better than it should. She tilted her head back as his tongue sent an urgent message to other parts of her body. Her nipples hardened and there was a warm ache in her pelvis.

Nico's hand moved to stroke her breast as his mouth found hers again, but when his hand settled on her thigh she stopped its upward movement with her palm.

"Why not? I've seen these legs before."

She stifled a groan. Pain could still throb there, but when she thought of the accident and her scarred body it became much worse. He hadn't seen her legs like this. They didn't look the same now.

"Sooner or later you'll tell me everything," he said.

Never. Trisha didn't talk about it with anyone. She remained silent, her gaze riveted to the trees in front of the car's window.

Nico sighed. "Okay, for now we'll pass on a rendezvous in a Ferrari *and* in the middle of a field, no less."

"I didn't stop the car in this field and don't remember asking to be in the car in the first place," she said. "Now I want to go back."

They sat, silent, for several minutes before the car rumbled to life, one grinding crunch and a thud sending it out of the field and down the road.

The drive back to the villa took place in the state of uneasy silence. She sat with her body pressed against the door, her gaze riveted to thin poplar trees outlined against the charcoal sky. And when he stopped in front of the villa, she jumped from the car without another word.

As he watched her disappear like some wily apparition, Nico cursed his desire for her, and lack of control. He had to ease up. She was tense, angry, and still so closed. Would she ever tell him about the other man? And those scars.

The one positive was he could still arouse her. Her mouth might say one thing, but her body told him something else. At least now he knew she and Luca weren't an item. Still, he had to sort things out himself, be sure of what he wanted before making another move—take some time to regain his equilibrium.

She was the only woman who could reduce him to this level of recklessness. He was renowned for rigid control in his business and personal lives. Women had always been accessories for him, except Trisha. She was the woman he'd taken to *his* bed, breaking his own cardinal rule and letting her do what no other female could—violate his private space. And his heart.

He'd begged her to move in with him, because he knew one night wouldn't be enough.

Truth be told, he didn't want another man to have her, was enthralled enough to think a live-in relationship would make a difference.

It didn't.

He met her, desired her, lusted after her for the six short months they were together—and repented at his leisure for that weakness after she betrayed him.

He slammed his palm against the steering wheel. How could an intelligent man be taken in like that? He was twenty-eight-years-old back then. Not a kid.

He sighed. She'd been an obsession, one that was now reigniting with a will of its own.

WHEN SHE GOT TO HER ROOM, TRISHA WILTED. WHAT A mess. She was in a vulnerable spot, locked into this contract, but the minute this was over she'd be on the first plane out of here.

She stared at the ceiling, a true testament to generations of Tuscan farmers. Its pale green surface embellished with a creamy plaster mural—grapevines interspersed with bowed olive trees.

She didn't know he was rich, back then. *How could she have?* He gave no indication of it. She'd have run in the other direction if she had known. Rich men were bad news, womanizers like her father who squandered his money and everyone else's.

She remembered meeting Nico in a Heathrow line-up, and after that didn't expect to ever see him again. She eventually realized he had access to resources most people didn't when he tracked her down in Milan, and caught up with her in the Piazza San Bablia.

Almost from the start her brain was mush around him.

"Signorina? Has no one warned you it's dangerous to wander about with your pocketbook in full view? These street thugs are slick and can rob you without your knowledge."

"Pocketbook?" For a minute she didn't understand. Then, "Oh, you mean my purse." She laughed as she reached a hand up to her shoulder just as he dangled her purse in her face. "And here I have your *purse*, but the thugs wouldn't be hanging around to return it," he'd said.

She remembered asking him how he found her to which he answered 'Did you think I would ignore our Heathrow meeting, never to see you again?'

And before she knew it they were together. A drink led to dinner, led to him helping her find a hotel room, led to him settling her in…

And so it went. Like Fatal Attraction in so many ways.

They couldn't keep their hands off each other. But great chemistry wasn't enough to withstand the trials their relationship faced, and it self-destructed when real trouble appeared.

NICO HAD VERY LITTLE SLEEP THAT NIGHT, AND WAS cranky when he walked into Luca's office the next morning, determined to get some answers.

Luca grinned and lounged back in his chair. "Aren't we the early bird. I have to say I was expecting you, but not *this* early."

"1 don't need tongue-in-cheek remarks from you right now. What were you trying to prove with Trisha?"

"Prove? Nothing. We're very good friends. That's all."

"I find that hard to swallow when you led me to believe otherwise."

Luca slapped a folder on his desk. "What's the difference? Trisha is nothing to you, is she?"

Nico gaped at his brother who was usually so even-tempered. "Luc, please." Surely he could depend on him for some understanding?

Luca leaned forward and planted his hands on his desk. "Aside from being one of the most kind, genuine people I know, Trisha has a Midas touch when it comes to events and that's why I hired her."

"And proceeded to let me think she was your woman."

"This is getting very strange, Nico. It's time you figured a few things out. If she's nothing to you leave it alone, but if you believe she can be a part of your life again, do something about it."

"I don't know what any of *this* is," Nico said. "It stunned me to see her here, shocked me even more to think the only woman I was ever serious with was now with my brother." He shrugged.

"But now you know she's only my friend." Luca blew out a deep breath. "All I can say is life's short, happiness fleeting, nursing old wounds and harboring grudges just plain stupid." He moved away from his desk. "Now, I have a business appointment and Trisha is in the ballroom with Madre if you want to see her."

Nico watched his brother leave. He'd come up with a strategy and now was the perfect time to move on it. With his mother there, Trisha would find it hard to rebuff the plan he was hatching. He headed for the ballroom.

Trisha motioned toward the alcoves. "Those will house the food and wine bars perfectly with lots of

mood lighting overhead and at the windows and—"
She paused. "Is that what you'd like, Annalia?"

"I think it will be perfect, Patricia. I trust you, and am happy with whatever you choose."

"Is this a closed party?" a husky voice asked.

"Of course not," Annalia replied as Nico walked towards them.

She lifted her cheek for her son's kiss and then he turned to Trisha, bending to bestow the same honor, although somehow he missed and licked his tongue along her sealed lips instead.

Infuriating man. She didn't want his mother thinking there was anything between them.

"Good morning. Sleep well?" Nico asked.

As his words hummed against her lips, she pulled her head back and their gazes connected. She knew the hot tinge of red showed on her cheeks.

"You still blush like a schoolgirl. When you did that I had half an idea what you were feeling." He winked. "But then again, you flush when you're aroused, too. It certainly revealed your mood when we made love all night long."

His whispered comment and the sexy tilt of his lips was too much. *I don't need this.* She turned to rejoin Luca's mother, but she'd disappeared with expedient ease.

As she looked around for Annalia, Nico's arm descended to her waist and his mouth met her ear.

"If it's any consolation my sleep wasn't great, too full of hot, intimate thoughts of you."

He reached for her hand, twining his fingers with hers, then turned to his mother who had quietly re-entered the room.

"Madre, don't you think it's time Trisha saw my farmhouse?"

Trisha wanted to avoid that. "I'm sorry, but I'm far too busy."

"Nonsense," Annalia said. "You have everything under control, the staff knows what to do, and you'll have your phone with you."

"Just once in your life give in gracefully," Nico whispered.

"My son will look after you." She smiled at Nico, and Trisha felt like a bird in a cage.

This family was good to her, and she respected their closeness. Now, Nico and his mother were watching, waiting, so she conceded defeat.

Was going off with him asking for trouble? Maybe. Was she curious about his Tuscan home? Absolutely. And she was older and wiser now, wasn't she? How much harm could there be in walking with Nico to his house?

As they strolled onto his home's wraparound veranda she breathed in air fresh with morning dew and the scent of cut grass. Scarlet poppies grew willy-nilly amidst the emerald foliage and the soothing scent of thyme and rosemary enveloped her. She opted to wait outside while Nico made their coffee, taking in this perfect antidote to her frazzled nerves. She lifted her head to the sun with a faint sigh.

Nico returned then, handing her a mug of coffee. "It's a wonderful place, isn't it?"

"For sure." She leaned over to gaze at the colors.

"When I'm home, I come out there to sit and just think," he said. "For me, it's the most relaxing place on earth."

"I get that." She lifted her head when she realized she was talking to the grass.

With a sudden move he stood behind her.

Now what? Second guessing him was exhausting. She glanced at him, and she understood. His gaze was focused on her back. Her top had crept up when she bent over.

He thumped his mug on the table and reached out to take hers. "I'm no longer willing to humor you about this. Your leg is scarred, so is your back, and don't dare try that damn bluff about a fall or a cut. You know I recognize the signs of a serious injury, so why bother trying to hide it from me?"

CHAPTER 4

The familiar pain drummed against her spine, but not like it did five years ago. Back then, it knifed through her motionless body.

When she'd come to, she was lying on a Milan street. It had started to rain, drenching her face and soaking her thin sundress. Someone covered her with a light blanket.

Now Nico's hand slid up and caressed her back, the feathery glide of his fingers tracing the scars. "Tell me."

She drifted back to that time. Sirens wailed and people screamed. Her past was returning, and she had to struggle with it—again.

He slanted his body against the railing. "Trisha?"

"I was hit by a car." What more could she say? The scars told the rest of the story.

"*Christo*. When?"

It was history, one that was directly linked to his

inability to believe in her. She'd never wanted to see him or hear his name after they'd parted, but now here she was—trying to have this conversation about her thorny past in which he played a starring role.

She stared at the beautiful landscape, mute, words numbed by her frenzied thoughts of so much physical pain, mental pain...

"When, Trisha?" he repeated.

"That night."

"*What* night?"

"Halloween, two years ago." Stupid questions deserved stupid answers.

A hard thump vibrated against the railing, buffeting the front of her body as she leaned there. She jumped back, startled, and glanced at him. The gold sparking in his eyes demanded a better response than the one she'd just given him. "It happened in Milan after I left your condo."

"And?"

"I wasn't paying attention when I stepped off the curb and did a polka with an oncoming car."

He flinched. "I don't find that amusing."

Of course he didn't, but she'd learned that flippant could get her through a lot of things in life.

"I know I wasn't kind, at the end, but..." He sighed. "I still think I should have known."

Not kind? And wasn't that an understatement. No, he shouldn't have known. A mere twenty minutes earlier he'd made it clear he never wanted to see her again.

She shrugged. "I was airlifted to Rome shortly after."

"I should have been notified."

"We were done, you'd washed your hands of me." She blew out a quivering breath. "And that nasty finale evened things out—upset when I got to Italy and upset when I left."

He bit out a low expletive. "I'll say this once more. I looked for you. I tried, and you didn't help by changing your name." His brows arched upward as he watched her. "What did you have to be upset about anyway? You were a young, smart, beautiful woman with your whole life ahead of you."

"My mother died two months before I arrived," she said.

"I'm sorry, that was patronizing. I had no idea."

"It certainly was, but you always patronized me."

He disagreed. "That's ridiculous."

"No, it isn't. I think the only time you were genuine was during sex, and if knowing that wasn't denigrating I don't know what is."

"I was crazy about you, but not always thrilled with the social scene. I'm sorry if that's how it came across… Now I understand better. You were trying to forget the pain."

"It didn't work."

"And I, astute person I'm supposed to be, missed all

of it when you needed me the most. Now it fits." He forked a hand through his hair. "How long were you in the hospital?"

"A month."

"How much plastic surgery did you need?"

"Enough."

"And physical therapy."

"That too."

"All of which took longer than a month, Trisha."

"Yes, but it brings back unpleasant memories."

She continued in response to his narrowed eyes. "I was transferred to Manhattan from Rome and spent a few more months in hospital there," she added. And surprise, *surprise*, they managed to put Humpty back together again."

"You're very good at joking about what destiny handed you."

"Nothing is ever accomplished by complaining, so I got on with my life."

"Why Manhattan? Before we met, you lived in San Francisco."

San Francisco was where she'd run to escape the embarrassment of her father's lewd and reckless behavior. "My cousin, Rachael, lives there, and I wanted to be close to family. It was also a good place to start over."

"You never told me about her," he said with a puzzled frown.

"You never told me about your family, either."

He held up his hands, palms facing her in apology. "Point taken, and I'm happy you had her." He smiled and draped an arm around her shoulders. "Let's walk, enjoy some sunshine, and then I'll make lunch."

It seemed her body was imprisoned by that arm and she couldn't seem to pull away. "I have things to do and really should get back."

"No, Madre assured us everything is under control for now."

"Do I have a say in this?"

"Not at the moment, no."

She slid from under his arm. "So let's get on with it, and then I'll have to get back to work."

NICO GRINNED AS HE WATCHED HER RETREAT. SHE MIGHT pretend an immunity to him but that was a lie. She could still fall apart in his arms. Maybe it was time for a refresher course. Two long strides down the steps, another two and he was in front of her. Without ceremony his hands clasped her startled face and his mouth met her gaping one.

TRISHA HAD NO TIME TO THINK BEFORE FALLING INTO that kiss with a fire that was astounding and scary. He took her with him as he sank to his knees while their tongues lingered in a slow dance. His hair-roughened thighs, in denim cut-offs, grazed her skin, and his heart pounded against her fist where it gripped his T-shirt.

He groaned, moving his hips against hers with sensual, shifting motions. When the evidence of his arousal pressed into her she panicked and pried her mouth from his, struggling to calm her breathing.

And just as upsetting was Nico's reaction to their temporary madness. He moved away, turning his back to her as he did. "A mutual-desire reminder," was all he said.

He wasn't even breathing hard. Was that kiss only about control? Was he toying with her? In one fluid motion she stood up and turned in the other direction. It was time to leave.

"And where do you think you're going, mia dolce amante?"

Trisha stopped and swiveled her head back to face him. His voice had that husky growl again and his breathing *was* labored. "I'm not your sweet lover."

"No, but I can hope, because if you don't put me out of this agony soon I'll have to commit myself to house arrest." He turned to face her. "I am becoming dangerous," he said as he strolled towards her. "But I do love that you want me, too." Then without any warning, he lifted her into his arms and began to walk to the other side of the house.

She hit his shoulder. "Nico, stop."

"Sssh, I think we both need to cool off, so let's do that."

Arguing was useless for now. She didn't want to love the feel of his hard muscles pressed against her. But she did. She didn't want to enjoy his musky scent. But she did. She didn't want to shiver at his warm breaths on her face. But she did. In fact, she didn't want to feel anything. But she did.

Then they hit the water with a loud splat. Without warning he'd dunked them in the pool. She surfaced and swam to the side, then rubbed at the sting of chlorine in her eyes before wringing some excess moisture from her hair.

"You, you…" she sputtered.

He was next to her then, the smirk on his face wider than the Arno River. She fisted her hand but he caught it before she could punch him.

"Non simpatico, cara. Not nice. Now go for a swim and cool off." He laughed when she pushed him away and began a lap of the pool, ignoring him completely. He did the same. Someone would have to carry her away on a stretcher before she'd admit defeat.

Finally, an arm snagged her waist and she was plastered against him again. She tried to ignore him by training her gaze on the hills surrounding them, but he was having none of that. "Look at me, Trisha."

Like she had a choice?

"Irritating bully," she mumbled.

"I heard you." He stroked her lips with his thumb. "You are so beautiful."

He broke the moment then, pulling her by the waist as he swam towards the seat in the azure-and-yellow-tiled pool's shallow end. "And I do hereby concede defeat in the swimming stakes. Satisfied?" he asked.

She leaned her face toward the sun. "I am."

"But you did have the advantage of lighter clothing," he said with a chuckle while hoisting himself from the pool and moving to one of the cabanas. He grabbed two large towels and short silk robes.

"Come and dry off, and then we'll go in for a shower."

"I don't think—"

"Then *don't* think. I have more than one bathroom which means you can have your privacy while I make lunch, and by then your clothes will be dry. It's settled."

"You are one bossy man. Did you go to bully school, or is it just a family trait?"

"Me? Never. I'm a creative problem solver which is essential to running a multinational corporation." He lifted her from the pool and draped a towel around her. "See? Problem solved.

So go dry off and put the robe on, bring me your wet clothing, and then we'll go inside."

The sun was hotter as they strolled back to the house. "Why aren't you a surgeon now?" she asked.

He stiffened. "I *am* a surgeon."

"But not a practicing one. Why the business persona?"

"I wish. A persona I could shed but this I can't."

That's ridiculous. You can do what you want."

"No, I can't. The livelihoods of many people and their families depend on me and my businesses."

She tut-tutted. "That's absurd. Hand it over to your executives, sit on the board in an advisory capacity, and go heal people if that makes you happy."

"Life isn't always so simple. We have to move on and I recognized when the time was right." He knew, in the weeks and months after she'd left on that final night, he had to change his life, to keep moving, try not to think or hope for something that would never be.

He stood back and touched his hand to her lower back as they reached his farmhouse steps.

Trisha stepped into his Tuscan home, onto pine-planked floors with a huge room off the front hallway. A floor to ceiling granite fireplace dominated one wall, its grey and earth-toned hues highlighted by the sun beaming through the adjoining window wall. Terra cotta pots filled with flowering plants in myriad shades of yellow, red, pink and blue overflowed the wide hearth.

"You like?"

She pulled in a deep breath, loving the muted scent

of beeswax lingering in the air. It reminded her of her grandfather's welcoming old house. Their gazes met.

"It's really very nice," she said. Quite an understatement, but it was a surprise.

She hadn't expected to see him in this setting with oxblood-leather sofas and oversized taupe chairs, all anchored in a grouping by a large pine steamer trunk. "I never would have expected the man I knew in Milan to end up in *this*."

"Why not? And what does *this* mean?"

"Your Milan apartment was trendy and ultrachic while this is warm and cozy."

"Ah, but the Milan apartment was a stopgap until I got through my surgery training."

She shrugged. "Was it? I didn't know." He hadn't shared either. She wasn't the only closed book back then.

"While I'm here I don't have to entertain business associates as I do in my other homes, so I decorated this place the way *I* wanted it—comfortable and warm." He smiled. "I did most of the renovations myself, too."

"Other homes?" How many did one person need? Had he turned into a globetrotting, party-circuit kind of guy? Why did that thought bother her? Because he was always so sensible when they were together. She *needed* his stability back then, although there were times it stifled her. She was so young.

"My travel schedule is relentless and I refuse to spend my life in hotels, living out of a suitcase, eating in intrusive restaurants where the paparazzi lurk, so yes I have other homes. It's necessary."

"But when I'm here I try, as much as possible, to file my business life in a totally different compartment." He grasped her hand and pulled her toward a winding staircase. "I'll show you where the bath is."

Sumptuous was the only word she could think of. An elongated alcove with overhead skylights held a curved soaker tub. Opposite that stood a massive shower wall with every type of high-quality faucet one could wish for as well as long marble seats, and a glossy black vanity with twin grey marble sinks. Shelves groaned under the weight of fluffy white towels and any toiletry a person could want.

Trisha resisted the urge to sink into a hot bath. Instead, she had a shower and sat on a small carved bench while waiting for her clothes to dry. *What was she doing here?* Not only had he hurt her, Nico was rich, out of her league. Truth be told, he always had been. Older, wiser, a lure for every avaricious female out there—and now she could add super high profile to his credentials, which certainly made him more untouchable. They inhabited different worlds.

Then there were the paparazzi he'd mentioned. They probably loved capturing him on film. He was such a stunning man. A magnet…

She would hate that kind of public life. Growing up with her father's overt vulgarity had taught her to dodge any kind of attention.

A knock on the door interrupted her thoughts. Nico, with her dry clothes.

"I'll see you downstairs when you're decent."

She dressed and sat for several minutes, trying to calm her frayed nerves.

"Trisha?"

His booming voice pulled her from her thoughts. *Show time.* She'd pretend her earlier behavior was temporary madness because more hurt was unthinkable. She couldn't go there again.

NICO WATCHED HER SKIP DOWN THE STEPS. SHE LOOKED like a little kid—face scrubbed shiny clean, hair swinging in a ponytail... He reached out to grasp her waist, swinging her down the last few steps and toward one of the side doors. He wanted to sit and feel her next to him.

He grinned at the question in her arched eyebrows. "The pizza's in the oven so I thought we could enjoy the sun while we wait." He drew her down on the garden swing, its cushioned seats splashed with a bright sunflower pattern, and began to push slowly.

SHE LET HIM CONTROL THE TENOR, BUT HAD TO ADMIT IT was also nice to sit like this. What could happen in broad daylight on a moving garden swing? Its rhythmic shifts and the sun warming her face soothed her tense muscles, and lulled her into a peaceful fog.

Her head nodded against his shoulder as his arm enveloped her waist and his lips moved against her forehead.

Then his fingers moved over her breast, slow and light.

She gasped when his thumb rubbed her nipple. "*Nico,* what are you doing?" *Dumb question, Trisha.*

"Whatever do you think I'm doing, bella?" His lips darted to her flushed cheek as his fingers continued to slide over her breast.

"No, we can't go there," she said. Someone had to be the voice of reason. "We tried this once and blew it. We also live in completely different worlds."

"You think we blew it?" His fingers brushed first one and then the other nipple. "If that's the case, what's this about?"

She moaned, a low sound that said she was losing this battle. "We were bad for each other."

"We made mistakes but we're smarter now."

What did that mean? Yesterday was gone. Rational thought ebbed when his mouth covered hers again— and doubt vanished as he fell back and pulled her down on top of him. The swing squeaked in protest while he moved her body back and forth against his, the friction increasing his arousal.

Luca's voice intruded then. "You at home, Nico?"

He pulled his mouth from hers, and vented a low Italian curse word. This smacked of bad timing for him, yet the interruption saved her from untold agony.

He straightened her clothes and jumped to his feet. "Did you and Luca plan this?"

"Don't be ridiculous. Why would we do that?"

"Si, that question requires an answer, doesn't it?" he said.

Luca strolled around the tall hedge that screened the swing. "Ciao," he said with a cheerful grin.

Ciao, indeed, Nico thought. Was little brother here to check up on them? Had the blonde been a cover so Luca could hide his true feelings for Trisha? Had he invited her to plan the gala because he didn't want to be away from her?

Men liked Trisha. He used to hate that. He was her first lover, and had sometimes wondered if she'd try it with another man and then just up and leave him.

She did try it, but it was him who ended their relationship when he found out.

"Enjoying the sun, are we?" Luca asked.

"We were, and now we're about to have lunch. Would you like to stay?" He might as well join them after ruining the mood here.

"That would be great. I have a few things to do in

Florence and really just stopped to hello on my way, but this saves me stopping for lunch, too."

"Madre told you Trisha was here, and you wanted to ask if she's interested in going with you, right?"

"Wrong on all counts," Luca replied, "but Trisha knows she is always welcome to accompany me wherever I go."

Nico turned and walked toward the house, but Luca caught up with him. "If I didn't know better I'd say you were jealous of me, your brother, which is too bizarre for even the most twisted mind."

"Don't push it, Luc. I'm not in the mood."

He'd just entered the kitchen when he heard other voices, and went to the window to check.

His sister, Isabella, was hugging Trisha while her three-year-old son, Andrea, clasped her legs in a death grip.

"What is this?" he asked.

Luca peered over his shoulder. "*This* is a close family. We adore the woman you let get away, and Andrea has certainly taken to Trisha these last few days." He chuckled. "I hope there's enough food for two more because I don't see you prying our nephew away any time soon."

Nico's gaze drifted to Andrea who now had Trisha engaged in what appeared to be a serious conversation. She was crouched down, smiling, listening to him as if they were the only people in the universe.

"Yes," he sighed. "Lots of pizza and salad for two more."

"I'm so sorry," Isabella said as they entered the kitchen. "I would never have stopped by if I'd known you were entertaining, but this bambino wanted to see you and…" Her voice trailed off.

Nico believed her. Luca was another story. He kissed her cheek. "I always love seeing you, Bella." Then he reached down, snatched Andrea up and tickled him into uncontrollable giggling—engaging him until Andrea tired of the game and asked when lunch was.

His gaze darted to Trisha. Why was she so quiet? She looked lonely and ill at ease. The urge to tell everyone to leave, to go and take her in his arms, to tell her, tell her… *what*? That she'd never again feel out of her depth in his home? What would that mean?

He compromised by bending down to kiss her forehead. Then he took her hand and led her to the large rectangular kitchen table, held out a chair to the right of his and waited while she sat, aware of Isabella's curious gaze.

Nico placed several large sliced pizzas, bowls filled with the mixed greens and reds of fresh vegetable salads, pitchers of water and juice, as well as plates, napkins and cutlery in the center of the table.

"Help yourselves, he said with a grin. "We're doing a casual lunch today."

Trisha seemed to relax after that. The informal

kitchen setting, gooey pizza and Italian enthusiasm worked their magic—and although Andrea monopolized her attention it was obvious she enjoyed his chatter.

"So are you into countdown mode yet, Patricia?" Isabella asked.

Trisha groaned. "Yes, and I couldn't survive without the staff."

Nico brushed his thumb along her cheekbone. "It will be perfect. Every time I am at the villa you're either on the phone or on a ladder," he said.

"And you are at the villa a lot these days, aren't you, Nico?" Isabella said.

He glanced at her, realizing she was right. "No more than usual."

"Of course not," she replied, grinning. "And now it's time I got this little tyke home for a nap. Luca?"

Luca pushed away from the table. "Yes, I have to get to Florence." Then… "Oh, Trisha, I almost forgot. There was a message for you to call Leo as soon as you can."

CHAPTER 5

"Sit, Trisha," Nico rested his palms on her shoulders when she tried to leave the table. How could he have thought all he needed with her was one last time for revenge? That was obviously not what he wanted, because he felt jealous of Leo, and had to find out more about the man.

"Do I have a choice?"

"Not at the moment, no." He sat in his chair and hooked one elbow on the back. "Who's Leo?"

"My right-hand at the office. I couldn't survive without him."

"I see." He didn't, but would find out more. And if Leo or any other son-of-a-bitch tried to take her away he would... what? His heart beat in sync with the pulsing in his brow.

What was he thinking? That she would be his again?

Yes. And this time, for as long as it lasted, he wanted exclusive rights.

"Nico?"

Did she just say something? He hadn't heard a word, because ever since seeing her again his libido ruled his brain. "Sorry, what was that?"

"I said thank you for the delicious lunch, and I have to get back."

He knew better than to push her. "It's too hot to walk now, so I'll drive you, and don't even think about arguing."

"Who would dare?"

"You, Trisha, would dare. In fact, when we were together you argued about many things."

"That was because I didn't always agree with you."

"You *never* agreed with me, but that's just one of the things that made our relationship so exciting."

Trisha ignored his comment as she pushed her chair back and moved to the door. He grinned as he watched her walk away, stared at her rigid back and sexy backside.

She was standing by his car when he caught up with her. "I swear you do what I least expect just to irk me," he said. "And there I was thinking I'd have to chase you down the road."

"Irk is such a sissy word. I prefer to think of it more as slow torture."

A low grunt erupted in his throat. "I can think of

other ways to offer that, so I suggest you get in the car before I haul you back to the house for a test run."

She moved.

Nico broke the silence on the drive back.

"I know about the rot Gina spread but it was false. I will be with whoever I wish, Italian or not, and want to ensure you understand there was never anything between Gina and me."

"Why tell me? It's none of my business."

"Will you stop with the stubborn routine and listen? She is very spoiled and needs to grow up."

"Save it for the gallery. I don't want to think about her sick neuroses."

A startled gasp escaped her when the car jolted to a stop and he walked around to open her door.

He leaned his head inside. "Come here."

She resisted with a shake of her head, but he reached for her hands and gently drew her from the car.

When her feet hit the ground he grasped her waist, pulled her tight against his chest and pushed their entwined bodies toward a nearby tree. He gritted his teeth. *How much longer could he stand this?* He breathed a silent prayer when her back met the grey bark of the towering maple.

"You challenged me, *always*. With every toss of that red mane and every flash of those blue eyes you challenged me." His forehead touched hers. "You *still* make my pulse roar and my blood sing, and believe me when I say Gina could never do that to me."

"She could never give me the same buzz with just one glance, or do *this* to me in the blink of an eye." He ground his hips against hers and watched her eyes widen at his obvious arousal. "Yes, cara, we still have this raging sexual hunger for each other."

She pulled away from him. "That doesn't mean we'll do anything about it. We tried and failed. I'm not up for more of the same."

Oh, it wouldn't be more of the same next time. It would be better, because *they* weren't the same people now.

And he was willing to wait.

He observed her rigid stance and compressed mouth. She was edgy, and her scars seemed to be a massive hurdle for her. She also had that emotional detachment he needed to respect. Now he understood how tough their break-up was for her. The ensuing accident hadn't only damaged her physically but, he suspected, mentally as well. He wondered if some other trauma happened earlier in her life which he didn't know about.

He stifled a shudder. The accident was his fault, if indirectly. He handled their parting terribly because of his own baggage, he realized now. He couldn't change any of that. All he could do was give her time, hope she'd adjust to his presence—and trust him again so they could revisit this hot passion still seething between them.

First, though, he'd have to accept her betrayal for what it was, the mistake of a confused young woman suffering from the recent loss of her mother.

Could he do that?

Trisha was still jittery the next morning. She'd never have dreamed all of this could happen, that she would ever see Nico again to begin with, or spend time with him, *and* grudgingly enjoy being with him.

This wasn't something she wanted now. She couldn't fix the past, and there was no place for Nico in her present or future.

So what was with this craving still trying to pull them together?

She was glad the gala was tomorrow, and then she'd be winging her way home—away from him.

Her day was shaping up to be trying, and Trisha needed every ounce of energy to cajole the creative element. She tasted cheeses the chef had chosen, sampled some of his outstanding dishes, watched the maintenance staff position the tables and gave them a thumbs up to the lights as they positioned them at the windows.

She was delighted with the glossy wine gift-bags

she'd ordered while still in Manhattan—a deep green emblazoned with the golden Bianchi logo. Rachael had put a bottle of the Bianchi Spirito Merlot in each bag, and now Trisha placed them on a long rectangular table near the exit for each of the departing guests to take one.

When she'd finished, Trisha leaned against the wall next to the table and took a drink from her water bottle.

"How's it going here?"

His voice startled her and the water she was drinking fast forwarded down her throat.

The bottle thudded to the floor as wheezing gasps replaced her normal breathing. The split seconds she spent trying to catch her breath seemed like an eternity. Memories of her accident and the sheer helplessness she'd felt rolled over her.

Nico moved across the room and was in front of her, his hands enclosing her shoulders. "You're okay or you wouldn't be able to take those breaths." He moved a cool palm over her clammy forehead. "Take it slow and breathe in from deep down."

She started to calm, following his instructions until her breathing settled. He wrapped his arms around her waist, and in her moment of relief she figured there was no other place she wanted to be. *Damn, what does that mean?*

Finally, Nico leaned back to gaze down at her, arms still linked at her waist. "You're very pale, so I'm getting you out of here for a bit."

"I can't. There's still a lot to do."

"Yes, you can." He touched her cheek with the back of his hand. "Doctor's orders."

They walked behind the villa, along a tree-lined path dotted with wild daisies. She glanced around, stunned at this outdoor haven. Gurgling water tumbled over a rock wall and into a small water garden. There was also a large seating area, BBQ and fire pits.

He took her hand and led her to a sofa with cushions that were the color of the noon sun above, and draped his arm around her shoulders. "I have a few things to say and some questions to ask."

"Am I going to like this?"

"I don't know, but I'm saying them anyway. This is long overdue." He closed his eyes while rubbing his temple. "I was distraught when it seemed you disappeared off the face of the earth. I was too rash and have lived with many regrets since."

"Oh, *Trisha?* Are you here?"

"I don't believe this," he muttered. "Who's that?"

"Leo?" She jumped up, her mouth agape.

"And I suppose you were expecting him?"

"Of course I wasn't."

"It's us, darling, here to save our star event planner."

"And what do you need to be saved from, *darling*?" Nico asked.

She glared at him just as Leo stepped into the clearing with—Rachael? Oh, oh. Trouble could follow when she showed up.

"Hello, sweetie," Leo said. "And look who I've brought with me. Surprise, right?"

Oh, yes. She nodded. "What are you doing here?"

"We thought you might need some help. When I called you with those business questions you sounded a bit frazzled."

Yes, but not so much that she needed them showing up here. They knew it, too. *What are they up to?*

And Leo only had a passing acquaintance with Rachael. How and why did they team up?

Nico stood and introduced himself, shaking hands. "I'll go and have the staff prepare two suites."

"No, we should be able to stay at one of the nearby B&Bs," Leo said, wincing when Rachael jabbed his side with her elbow.

But Nico had already disappeared.

"Don't be silly, Leo," Rachael said. "Look around you. I *want* to stay here. It'll be the best vacay I've ever had."

"And I want to know what's going on," Trisha said. "So talk."

"Don't ask me," Leo replied as he rubbed his ribs.

Trisha glanced at her cousin. "Rachael?"

"I don't need that hoity-toity look from you," she replied.

Trisha pinched the bridge of her nose and drew in a soothing breath. "I'm not asking again."

"Well, after checking into Nico's background I realized he was from *here* and not Milan, and—"

Leo took up the story. "I'd just hung up from talking to you and had a bad feeling. You didn't say it, but I thought there was more to your stress than an event you could normally handle with your arms tied behind your back."

"And I dropped in to see if Leo had heard from you." Rachael flapped a hand in air. "So here we are. Your moral support."

"Did you ever think I might not need it?"

"Of course you do," Rachael said. "Nico is here. The man of your dreams. The one who disowned you, remember? How could you *not* need us?"

Nico re-appeared then with a staff member. "Cosima will show you where to go. After a long trip you might want to rest. A lunch will be delivered to your suites."

"I'll go and help them," Trisha said.

But Cosima was already leading them away.

Nico crossed his arms. "Did you think you'd get away that easily?" He stifled a grin. There he was worried about Leo's relationship with Trisha, until he saw the man's pink and purple polka-dotted bowtie and pink-striped jeans. At least his shirt was a plain color, if a bit bright. His fear of that competition was well and truly terminated.

He watched as she rubbed her hands up and down

her bare arms and stared at the treed horizon. She was still nervous, and he'd need loads of resolve to get through to her. Patience wasn't one of his stronger qualities but for her he'd wait. Hadn't he thought about her for five years? Yes.

"Nico, I have a lot of work to do before tomorrow."

"But you have Leo to help you now."

"He'll just get in my way."

"You said he was indispensable."

"He is, at the office."

"And?"

"I've never seen him and Rachael together, but if bedlam tends to follow her I suspect trouble when they show up together." She released a shaky breath. "I don't need that right now."

IT WAS JUST PAST MIDNIGHT AND TRISHA WAS STILL IN the ballroom when a raspy voice interrupted her reverie.

"Ciao, cara."

Surprised, she turned too quickly, and jerked her neck. "Ouch," she muttered as pain shot down her back.

He was at her side in an instant. "Will you *stop* twisting your limbs like that?"

Trish glanced at him, at the sexy dark stubble on his

jaw. It used to feel so good when she rubbed her fingers there…

Past tense, Trisha. She had to keep reminding herself of that since seeing him again.

"What are you doing here?"

"I couldn't sleep."

"Sorry, but I'm busy and don't have much time to chat."

"No one is ever too busy, Tish."

"Please don't call me that." *Please.*

"Why? Don't you think we can work on our past?"

She shook her head, her gaze riveted to her sneakers. "No, I don't."

"Can't you let me try to fix what's broken?"

She stifled a distressed groan. She was broken. Her body was broken. No one could fix any of that. "I'm afraid my scars are here forever, and the plastic surgeons who worked to improve them have exhausted their abilities."

"This isn't about your physical scars. I'm talking about the emotional ones."

She crossed her arms at her waist. "The two are inextricably linked and will be for the rest of my life, so there's no sense talking about it."

He grasped her arm and pulled her into an alcove. "Do you find relationships hard, or are you just not interested in ever having one?" He winced. "Or maybe not having one with me again? Is that it?"

Relationships *were* hard. First, there was her father,

and then this man and his inability to trust her, which led to their nasty parting. She glanced at him, at the questioning frown on his face—a face, she was loath to admit, that had invaded her dreams far too often.

"Trisha?"

She usually repressed the icy despair of her past, but now those memories rattled in her brain like a pocketful of loose change needing to be spent. "My father unzipped his pants for any female who came along, until he finally ran off with a girl more than half his age. She was the older sister of a good friend of mine. We lived in a small town and it was humiliating. I blame him for my mother's ill health and early death. I hated my father. Hated him, hated his name, too, and despised having that name myself."

He hugged her as his chin stroked her hair. "I'm sorry you had to live through that, but not every man is the same."

"I didn't have much of a role model to guide me, so it's easier to avoid entanglements with the opposite sex."

"You tangled with me."

"Yes, and look where that got me."

"Look where it got *us*, cara."

"Do you know what, Nico? It doesn't matter anymore."

"It does." He bent his head until their gazes locked.

The bright-green flashes in his eyes excited her, even as she knew his wily brain was at work trying to probe her innermost feelings. "Our lives are in different places now."

"Not when I feel like this they aren't." He ground their hips together. "I know you feel the same," he said, skimming his lips over hers, "but I can wait if I have to."

A female voice interrupted them. "This looks wonderful, Trisha. Totally awesome."

"And based on our interfering families I'll be waiting a long time," he murmured in her ear.

Trisha peeped around his shoulder to see Rachael standing there, her head bobbing about as she examined the room.

"Oh, hi, Nico. I didn't think I'd see you here at this hour. I guess you couldn't sleep?"

He laughed. "Sleep is overrated when I can be here instead."

Trisha stifled a groan. *Who was Rachael trying to kid?* She wanted to check things out, to see if Nico was here —and found them in a clinch. She'd tried to keep her cousin and Leo busy at the winery so they wouldn't cross paths with Nico, but Rachael's natural curiosity would never leave it at that.

"I wanted to check and see if you need us for anything else. Leo's going to handle the traffic tomorrow as we discussed and he has a few young men to help. I'll be at the door with two of the winery staff to take invitations, show them to the coat check and direct them here."

Trisha nodded. "I'll have some last-minute things to

do in the morning, so it'll be great having you and Leo here."

"Yes, we won't be at the winery with nothing to do. We know you sent us there today to keep us away from Nico," Rachael replied, winking at him.

Trisha couldn't deal with any more of this. "I'll see you here at seven a.m.?"

Rachael hesitated, then nodded. "With bells on."

Trisha watched her cousin leave. She loved Rachael, but she could be a handful at times.

Nico didn't move his arms from her waist the whole time Rachael was here, and now they loosened as he leaned back to look at her. "What did you do after you healed from the accident?"

"Why does that matter?"

His hands moved to cup her bottom, his touch light as he squeezed. "Humor me."

Spasms of heat coiled along her spine. She didn't want him to know she'd never forgot his touch. "I studied, completing my MBA, and then travelled, learning French and Spanish along the way. When I returned home I started Abbott Affairs."

"Why event management?"

Of course he would ask that. She used to go out to jazz clubs with his cousin, Maria, while he studied. He'd called it partying. But it wasn't. She and Maria both loved music. That was all. It was just a break from the mundane.

"Do you think it's more than just parties?" she asked.

He grinned, his hands moving up to her waist again, the fingers beginning a slow dance up and down her back. "I do."

"Well, I guess it's because I'm never bored. Each event is unique, a challenge, but then it's over and I move on to a different one."

"Can't let grass grow under your feet, *hmm?*"

No, she couldn't. "I like moving on, not stagnating, meeting lots of different people."

"And not forming any lasting attachments by the sound of it."

"I don't have the time."

"Everyone needs time for family and friends."

"But I'm not everybody."

He pulled a face. "No, you certainly aren't. You're still the same puzzle you always were, but this time around I'm learning how to decipher you."

"Why bother? I'm leaving here soon."

AND HE'D BE RIGHT BEHIND HER. HE'D THOUGHT ABOUT that and made some decisions of his own. He could work from Manhattan as well as anywhere. Although the past was dead, he felt like today was full of potential he would never have dreamed possible a short week ago.

She might have been a mystery from the outset but the passion between them was real—it survived and even flourished during their years apart. And wasn't it her hidden depths that had intrigued him, sucked him in like a greenhorn on his first date?

Yes, and he hadn't done enough to break through her barriers. He judged her based on his experience with a woman from his past, one who partied and shopped too much even as she lusted after his money. In that, at least, he hadn't been fair to Trisha.

He pulled in a deep breath. He let anger bleed him dry for five years, believed she'd run off with someone else, when really she'd suffered from that horrific car accident. She was quite a woman in so many wonderful ways. "I wish I could play that scene again, cara."

"There were definitely lots of them," she muttered.

His arms tightened at her waist. "I'm talking about the one where I ended our relationship." He grimaced. "I behaved like a schoolboy when I kicked you out into the rainy night, and then you had that dreadful accident."

"Nico, I have a lot to finish up here and this conversation is futile."

"No, it isn't, and we still have a lot of talking ahead of us."

"If it was meant to be it would have happened."

"It did happen, and it was incredible. We couldn't keep our hands off each other. Dio, we were between the sheets a few hours after we met."

"I suppose you thought I was a cheap tart."

"Did you ever once hear me complain? I was *there*, remember? And just as keen."

"Don't be so crass."

"That wasn't what our relationship was about, Trisha. What we shared was torrid, incredibly sensual and exciting, but never crass."

"Hello? Is someone still here?" Luca's voice came from the hallway outside the ballroom.

Trisha stepped away from him just as Luca appeared.

Nico blew out a rough breath. "Christo," he muttered.

"Oh, surprise, surprise. You're *both* here," Luca said with a slow wink.

"Where did you blow in from?" Nico asked.

"Media interviews at the winery were today. They went well, thanks to Trisha and her team's hard work. So everything's a go for tomorrow. Also, I've confirmed our Russo cousins will be here.

"Ah, the successful brothers from Puglia." A dynamic pair who produced and marketed superb olive oils. Many women had tried in vain to get them hitched.

His more immediate problem, however, was whether one of those successful men-about-town might want Trisha before he could win her back.

Trisha appeared in the ballroom at six the next morning. The kitchen would be humming to ensure perfection for the gala's food stations. The chef was preparing many dishes but there'd also be fruits and assorted cheeses, breads, oils, olives… Every food and garnish imaginable to complement the Bianchi wines. The Spirito Merlot would be introduced at midnight.

She poked her head into the kitchen, and out as quickly. The sous chef's clipped voice and gesticulating arms told her to stay away.

Rachael and Leo showed up an hour later. "We're here," Rachael said. "Ready to roll up our sleeves and help."

How could her cousin always sound so cheerful? Trisha was more serious, but life hadn't been as kind to her. Every day she tried to put the jagged pieces of her soul back together, and thought she was finally winning—until she'd met Nico again.

The maintenance staff had already done a test run with the lights. The chandeliers would be dimmed, but along the room's vast length brighter lights would beam down on the food and wine bars, and the tenor's dais. The lighting was a go.

The staff had also draped filmy fabric from the chandeliers to the outer corners of the room, the Bianchi logo twinkling along its length.

"Everything seems to be ready and I'll be glued to my phone, so it appears you're both off the hook for now."

It was six p.m. when she re-appeared, dressed in a silk gown, ivory with Swarovski crystal beading on the bodice. Her maternal grandmother's amethyst necklace sat at her throat, and purple stilettos added a fun touch that made it easier to converse with the many tall Italians she'd seen since arriving here.

She and Rachael stood near the entrance where Luca and his parents were welcoming the guests when Rachael nudged her. "*Look* at those males talking to Luca."

Trisha squirmed. "What is it with you and elbowing people?"

"I only do it when I'm lost for words."

"*You*, lost for words? When?"

"Right now, because I'm stunned by the eye candy on display."

Trisha followed her gaze, glancing at the door just as Luca caught her eye, and after a word with his parents he walked toward her, the two handsome men in tow.

"I want you to meet my cousins, the eminent Russo brothers," he said. "This is Domenico, Dom to his friends."

Trisha reached out to shake Dom's hand, but he wrapped an arm around her shoulders instead. "You have been hiding this beauty from me, Luc?"

"No, Trisha lives in Manhattan and is staging this event."

"Ah, I can see I'll have to make more trips to Manhattan."

Luca groaned. "And this," he continued with a slash of one hand, "is Dom's more reserved brother, Clemente, also known as Clem."

Clem nodded his head, grinned and sidled up to Rachael just as Nico materialized.

"Well, if it isn't our cousins in the flesh." Nico shook Clem's hand, then reached for Dom's while snaking his other arm around Trisha's waist, and drawing her tight to his side. "I also make many trips to Manhattan."

Trisha pulled away to free herself from the male posturing, and the heat of Nico's body pressing against hers. "I have to work," she said as she excused herself.

But with the superlative Parrettini staff, she realized there wasn't a lot left to do until they neared the midnight hour, so she mingled.

The Italian tenor in a dark tux serenaded the crowd. His rich voice reverberated through the room, and the crystals hanging from the chandeliers tinkled in time. Trisha stood by one of the alcoves, mesmerized by that voice with only the violins backing him up now, when Dom appeared next to her.

"Can I ask you something, Trisha?"

She nodded. "Of course."

"Are you and Nico in a relationship?"

Whoa. "Why would you ask that?"

He smiled. "Because if you aren't I'll ask you out on a date."

She gulped to clear the lump in her throat. "We were once, but that was years ago."

"So can I call you when I'm in Manhattan?"

She shrugged. "Dom, I'm not dating at this point in my life. It's not personal. I'm just busy, and don't have time for relationships."

Rachael sidled up next to her, interrupting their conversation. "It's long overdue, and you need to make time."

How did that woman manage to appear at the most inconvenient times?

"Leave it alone, Rach."

Dom's gaze darted from Trisha to Rachael, and back again. "I guess I should leave it too?"

A husky voice replied. "That might be best."

Nico.

"Of all the people in this room, the three of you have to stand by me to what? Nag for sport?"

Nico grinned with a flash of white teeth while Rachael and Dom managed to vanish.

"It's just us now. Ignore everyone else and dance with me. Tenors croon out some of the *best* songs." He gripped her hand and led her onto the floor.

There were so many people around that Trisha knew she had to do this with a smile.

He twined his arms around her waist and shuffled in place. The only tangible movement was his lower body brushing against hers—his aroused lower body.

"Did I tell you how stunning you look in that dress?"

His warm breaths pulsed against her brow. "Thank you."

"And those shoes are definitely sex on heels."

"Nico, can we just get through this dance without a hassle?"

"How is this a hassle?" He leaned back and his hand met her chin, tilting her face up until their gazes met. "Maybe because you feel more for me than you'll admit, even to yourself?"

She didn't reply, twisting her head around to survey her surroundings instead.

"When tonight is over," he said, "we're going to talk,

away from here, from people and distractions. Just us, cara."

Why bother? It wouldn't solve anything. "It never worked before." She pulled away from him and lost herself in the crowd.

AT EXACTLY TWENTY MINUTES BEFORE MIDNIGHT THE staff opened the terrace doors so people could move outside. Trisha had organized the wine so it was ready to serve before the midnight hour. The terrace looked perfect. At one end, the wine was displayed on glass shelves, the spotlights above showcasing bottles of the dark-ruby wine with their sparkling golden labels. The swirling "B" of the Bianchi logo was reproduced in an oversized version, and several of them hung from the beams and swayed in the gentle breeze.

As waiters finished serving the guests, a boom lit up the night sky with the gold logo and smaller ones radiating from it. Red starbursts added to the fireworks show as they moved in the background before crackling away into the night sky. That was when Luca moved onto the dais next to the wine. He raised his glass before taking a drink. "To our newest family member, the Bianchi Spirito Merlot," he said to the "oohs" and "aahs" of approval as the guests tasted their wine.

While Trisha took a sip she noted Nico tipping his glass to her.

Things were wrapping up at two a.m. when Dom approached her. "Could you give my cousin a break and listen to him?"

What was this about? She just met Dom that evening and he was giving her advice? Then it struck her. This smacked of Rachael's well-meaning interference. "What did my snooping cousin tell you?"

"Enough for me to know you and Nico need to talk."

"No, Dom, I need to get home to Manhattan."

"And I'm sure my cousin will follow you." He grinned. "If I don't stand a chance with you it might as well be my cousin you're with." He grinned. "I can definitely vouch for him."

She wasn't going there. "It was great to meet you, Dom."

"Oh, we'll see each other again, Trisha." He blew her a kiss. "Soon, yes?"

WHEN THE LAST GUEST HAD DEPARTED TRISHA LEFT THE ballroom and moved down a long hallway towards her suite. She was delighted everything went off without a hitch. The event was perfect.

The minute she closed her door, she kicked off her shoes. These stilettos pinched without mercy.

"Too bad the shoes have to go."

Her head jerked up. "What are you doing here, Nico?"

"Not many people could pull off purple shoes with that dress, cara."

Trisha crossed her arms, mute. She didn't want him here ruining the pleasure she felt from the evening's success.

"I warned you we were going to talk." He gestured to an adjacent chair with one hand. "Sit down, Trisha."

Her hands met her hips. "I want you to leave. You have no right to be here."

"You'd rather sit on my lap while we talk?"

She rubbed her forehead. The nagging ache wasn't about to ease any time soon. She slumped in a chair.

"Good girl."

"I'm not a girl."

A groan rumbled in his throat. "I *know*."

She didn't like the green fire sparking in his eyes, or his relaxed sprawl that said he wasn't leaving any time soon. "What do you want?"

"Is that a real question?"

"Yes."

"I have to know what happened to us. Why did you need another man?"

"Nothing like getting right to the point, Nico."

"*Why*, Trisha?"

"I didn't need another man."

"Christo, I found you hiding condoms. Our bed was rumpled like there'd been a sex orgy there."

She sighed. The truth wasn't always pretty. "It wasn't me."

"Then who?"

"Does it matter anymore?"

"It damn well does. I won't leave until you tell me the truth."

The ache throbbed behind her eyes now. "You didn't want the truth then. Why now?"

"Trisha?"

She closed her eyes, thinking… It was so long ago. It couldn't hurt anyone if she told him. "It was Maria."

"My cousin?"

She nodded.

"Why? She was a blissful, soon-to-be-married woman."

"And she's now happily married to that fiancé. It was a fling. She said she needed to let loose before settling down forever. He was an old boyfriend."

"And that makes it better?" His voice shook. "You took the blame for that. I treated you like a—"

"Whore was one of the things you called me at the time."

"You don't have to keep reminding me." He jumped up and began to pace. "I wish I could change it, have wished it every day since the words left my mouth."

"But you can't. You're a closed, intolerant rich man

who, if you ever settle down, needs a woman whose idea of a relationship is spending your money."

"I had one of those before I met you, was engaged to her, in fact, and thought I loved her. She showed me no such thing existed."

He was engaged before her?

"And you didn't think I deserved to know that? You've just proved my point. You *are* a closed man." And she was too tired for any more of this. "Nico, I have a bad headache, I still have my evening gown on, and dawn isn't far away. I need some sleep."

He stilled. "Are you ever going to give me another chance?"

"It's impossible."

"I know I was unreasonable."

"You were beyond that."

He slipped in front of her, his unblinking gaze boring into hers. "Yes, I was horrible, but I want us to try again, and I need your forgiveness first."

"Why bother? If it's just sex you want you can get that anywhere."

"That's not all I want."

"You just said you'd found out love didn't exist, so sex must be all that's left."

"And you're determined to burn me at the stake, aren't you?"

"No, I'm trying to get on with my life and accept my scarred body for what it is."

He scraped a hand across the back of his neck. "I don't care if you have a few little scars."

A forefinger tapped her mouth for a millisecond. "Read my lips. They. Are. Not. *Little*." And if he'd trusted her more she wouldn't have any. Not one. So there. She did blame him.

His eyes were sparking gold now, and Trisha couldn't handle anything else for one night. "Please, I can't think until I get some sleep."

He didn't move or speak for several minutes, staring at her from the blank mask of his face. "Promise me we'll talk in the morning?" he asked quietly.

She nodded. Anything to get him out of there.

Nico leaned against the wall outside her suite, his heart beating like a drum in a marching band. Since they'd parted five years ago, blaming her fought hard with wanting her, and worrying about her. But when they were together she never gave him a reason to distrust her. Never. Now he knew the truth, and felt shame, remorse. The way he'd treated her and what he'd said was inexcusable.

Everything she said was true. The horrifying accident and her resulting scars, the long recovery... His fault. All of it. And she'd just been protecting *his* cousin.

Where would the future lead? He didn't know. He

had to worry about yesterday first, try to drill through her rigid defenses before he could consider getting her to think positively about tomorrow.

TRISHA FOLDED HER GOWN INTO THE SUITCASE AND zipped it shut. There was no sense hanging around. The event was a huge success, but it was over. Time to go home. She'd do her final report there and email it to Luca.

She strolled over to the window, looking out at the Tuscan countryside she'd come to love in the short time she was here. Dawn was starting to break, the pink-streaked sky highlighting the green vine-covered hills. She'd miss this.

A FEW HOURS LATER SHE WAS IN THE AIRPORT DEPARTURE lounge. Renting that car was genius.

The Parrettinis had said their staff could run errands for her but she'd persevered, and was glad she did. The rental was useful then and also became her escape route. She wouldn't have been able to get a cab out there in the middle of the night.

Before boarding her flight, she texted Luca to tell him she'd left. It was easier for everyone to find out afterwards. She bit at a thumbnail as a lone tear trickled along her cheek. She'd miss those wonderful people.

But she would finally be able to pay off the last of her father's debts. She'd refused to let her mother carry that burden. She hadn't been well and didn't need the added stress—not after the way he'd treated them.

Her thoughts drifted to Nico. Five years ago, she wanted it to work with him, but it took seeing him again to realize some things weren't meant to be. She didn't do relationships—and observing the happiness in the Parrettini family cemented her belief she could never give that or be that to someone else.

She had no experience being part of a solid family unit. All she felt, she realized now, was this long-buried distrust and humiliation that came from living with a worthless father who'd only ever thought of his own selfish needs. Happy families weren't built from experiences like hers.

NICO WALKED INTO LUCA'S OFFICE THE NEXT MORNING. "Have you seen Trisha yet?"

"No, but I haven't been looking for her. Have you checked with Madre?"

"Yes, and the staff."

Luca picked up his phone when it beeped, and stared at the message. "Oops, she's not here."

"Where is she?"

"Gone. Flew the coop. Ran away. Fled—"

"Nico raised his hands. "Okay, I get it."

"I'm delighted you do."

"But *why*? We were going to talk this morning," Nico muttered.

"I guess that wasn't on *her* to-do list."

"Cut the sarcasm. Is she headed back to Manhattan."

Luca tilted his chair back and nodded. "She is. So what are you going to do about it? Follow her or ignore her for the next five years, maybe overlook the fact she even exists?"

"I don't know. I'll have to think about it."

"And where has that got you in relation to Trisha?" Luca asked.

"She's difficult and so is our history. There are issues to tackle with her. I wasn't kind to her at the end, and I'm not sure she'll ever come around."

"And will you?"

Nico massaged the knots of tension in his neck. "What's that supposed to mean?"

"That you have a chip on your shoulder the size of a small country, and it's all because of that spoiled girl you once thought you loved."

"I did love her."

"I never believed that, and you have to settle two things before you see Trisha again. First, you have to think back to your marriage that wasn't. If you had married that woman do you think her money-hungry silliness would have made you happy and led to forevermore? If not, it was never love to begin with, and you have to bury it for good. And second, you can't play games with Trisha. She isn't the person you knew before. Your break-up and the accident changed her.

And both were his fault. He blew out a long breath before turning to leave the office, phone to his ear, low voice curt. "I want to fly to Manhattan today. When can we expect a time slot?"

HE HAD LOTS OF TIME TO THINK DURING THE FLIGHT. What *did* he want?

Looking back, he felt the same betrayal when he'd entered his and Trisha's bedroom as he had standing alone at that altar. Still, Luca posed a good question. Would that marriage have lasted?

No. Angelica *was* shallow and he did have a lucky escape, although the indignity of it haunted him for a long time. But that was an issue of pride, not loss.

No more. He came from a happy family and wanted that for himself someday. He'd judged Trisha rather than listen to her explanations, while berating himself for supposedly making the same mistake a second time. He didn't give her a chance.

Could he ever forgive himself for that, and for the accident she had after he threw her out?

Better yet, what would he say to her now? He couldn't fix the past, but the future was full of possibilities. Maybe if he came to Manhattan often enough they could date, get to know each other again. Yes! That was a perfect plan, but he had to tread carefully with this changed Trisha.

Nico picked up the squat glass of Scotch he'd ignored until now, and held it up in a toast to a future he was just beginning to glimpse.

TRISHA COULDN'T BELIEVE WHAT HER ASSISTANT WAS saying. "You're telling me a company that runs a dating-for-sex service wants us to do a celebratory event for those who found *mates?*"

Did she need this one day post Tuscany?"

"That's the gist of it, although it isn't just dating for sex."

"Tell them no."

"There's a huge amount of money involved here, Trisha."

"I don't care, and wouldn't take it even if we were desperate for business, which we aren't."

The next few days were a blur. Things were hectic at the office and she was working long hours. She wondered why she hadn't heard from Rachael who had to be back in Manhattan by now. Was she up to something? If so, Trisha hoped it didn't involve her.

She was filling her dishwasher on a Saturday afternoon not long after she'd returned to Manhattan when the doorbell rang. She stilled. The doorman always called up when there were visitors.

She checked the peephole. Rachael.

"Where have you been?" she asked the minute the door opened.

Rachael shrugged. "Around."

"That's not very enlightening."

She shrugged again while walking into Trisha's foyer. But as she entered, a man slipped from beside the door where he'd stood, out of sight, and walked in behind Rachael.

Nico.

"Excuse us, Nico. I have to talk to Rachael."

"Oh, I'm not going anywhere, cara."

"What do you think you're doing?" Trisha asked when she cornered Rachael in the kitchen.

"You left without a word to those folks who were so kind to you, so I decided it was time for you to be polite and face some of the music."

"You had no right to do that."

"I did. I refuse to be your intermediary forever, and the best way to end this impasse is to bring you and the love of your life together."

Trisha's forefinger touched her lips. "*Sssh!* He'll hear you."

"Trust me, he won't overhear us in such a large condo."

"And he is *not* the love of my life."

Rachael blew out a frustrated breath. "Believe what

you want, but he's here now and you have to talk to him."

"I can't do this, Rach."

"Can't or won't?"

She bit at the corner of her lip. "Both."

"Well, Nico isn't a man who'll leave because *you* want him to."

She looked at her tattered jeans and faded T-shirt. "I'm a mess."

A laugh gurgled in Rachael's throat. "I don't think he'll care."

"You shouldn't have done this, Rach."

To which her cousin curved an arm through Trisha's and strolled into the living room. "This is where I bid you both adieu," she said with a grin and a wink. Then she was gone.

CHAPTER 7

Nico turned from his contemplation of the skyline. "I'm impressed, cara. A midtown Manhattan condo. This is swish."

"I'm looking after it for a friend." She slumped in a chair. "What do you want, Nico?"

"Several things." He began to pace. "First, Luca told me he planned your Tuscan trip before he ever met you. Did you know that?"

"That's ridiculous."

"It's true. He was trying to make me jealous, so fired me up by bringing you back into my life, and it did the trick." He heaved a ragged sigh. "I was spinning in so many directions."

She crossed her arms. "Why would he do that?"

"Because he believed we had unfinished business."

"We finished in Milan."

"What I did can never be undone, but now I realize

the shame I felt by being left at the altar invaded our relationship. I treated you horribly."

She stared at him, her silence filling the room with a sound of its own—the implicit seething of stress, anger and sadness.

"Will you say something?" he ground out. "I can't talk to dead air."

"What do you want me to say?"

"That you'll go out to dinner with me when I'm in the city."

Trisha walked toward the fireplace, staring at her mother's little crystal wishing well. A wonderful symbol of hope for those who believed. "What do you suppose dinner would accomplish?"

"A better understanding of one another."

"Why?"

Nico moved with the stealth of a lion on the hunt, wrapped an arm around her waist and turned her towards him. "Why not?"

"I don't date, Nico. Not anyone, and that includes you. It's not for lack of interest from the men I've met in my life. It's just not for me."

"Is that because of our breakup, your scars—or both?"

"The scars don't help."

Nico fell to his knees in front of her, undid the snap on her jeans and eased them down. When her thigh was exposed, he touched it with his lips, let them roam there in a tender salute. "I love your body, and a few scars don't change that."

Trisha shuffled back while pulling her jeans up. "Please don't."

HE STOOD, STARTLED, WHEN HE NOTED HER REDDENED cheeks. That she could get embarrassed after the intimacies they'd shared didn't just crank up his libido —it uncovered a warm feeling, one of completeness he'd never allowed himself to feel after his nuptials fiasco.

Now he thanked his old girlfriend for leaving him at the altar. If she hadn't, he'd never have met this amazing woman.

Christo, he wanted more than occasional dating. He wanted forever with her.

He touched his lips to her brow, reached for her hand and led her to a linen-covered sofa where he pulled her down next to him, and caged her with an arm at her waist. His gaze held hers. She was tense, but he forged ahead regardless. He needed to make this right.

"First, let me say when I tried to hire your company here in Manhattan last week, I didn't want you for just sex. I wanted a date, but still think that sex-for-dating scenario could have been hot, cara."

That got a reaction.

Her eyes widened as she gasped out an unintelligible sound.

"That was you?"

"It was, but I had plans to work on the date first. The rest was a dream fantasy, when really I would have been happy to begin with a smiling Trisha."

"I was smart enough to veto your sex-for-dating idea."

"Yes, but then I had to find another way to see you, so I called Rachael."

"Why didn't you call me?"

"Let's face it, Trisha. I wasn't sure you wanted *that* face-to-face after the way you vanished from Italy without a word."

"So you resorted to subterfuge?"

"Yes, and look at me now. It worked."

"The ball's in your court, Nico."

He pulled in a deep breath. "You might not be ready for serious but I am."

"When we were together you were a breath of fresh air, and despite our differences I loved coming home. Every relationship has growing pains and that's how I looked at ours. But that day in Milan, when I walked into our bedroom, it felt like I was standing alone at the altar again, and I reacted without thought."

"You were a raging maniac."

"Yes, and I want to spend the rest of my life making it up to you."

Her startled breath galvanized him.

"I love you, Tish, and will forever. I want it all. You

and me and several children we can love and spoil. "How does that sound to you?"

"It's impossible. Geography alone is a huge issue."

"No, it isn't. I can work from Manhattan as easily as anywhere and when I travel you'll come with me. But right now all I want to know is how you feel about me, *us*."

"Please say something," he muttered to the blank mask of her face.

Nico wasn't expecting her to start crying, but she did.

He pulled her onto his lap, touching his lips to her damp eyelids, to her cheek where he traced the path of her tears. "Talk to me. Tell me I can make this better, make us whole again."

"I'm scared."

"I'm not like your father. I'll love you with my heart and soul."

"That's not it."

"Then what is *it*?"

"I don't know how to be a family, how to make a stable family unit."

"Is that what you want, cara? Me, noisy kids, and however many animals they ask for?"

"I'm not sure."

"You had a secure family unit with your mother, and it was *you* who made her life happy and trouble-free after your father, so forget those negative thoughts." His lips touched hers. "We can do it, and if you have questions ask me." He smiled. "We'll learn together. How does that sound?"

She nodded, her sobs ebbing as he hugged her against him.

"But first I want us to be together as two—to purge old ghosts and spend quality time with each other. Start making happier memories. What say you?"

"Yes, we could try."

"Try is a sissy word and I'm not a sissy kind of guy, cara. We're going to rock our marriage and parenthood. And that's a promise."

EPILOGUE

Trisha stared out at the hills of green vines dotted with clusters of dark purple grapes. Tuscany. The perfect place for her engagement party. She was back in the same bedroom she'd used a year ago during the wine launch. Who'd have dreamed so much could happen? That she and Nico would be able to rekindle their love. They spent the last year dating, alternating between Manhattan and Tuscany.

Nico presented her with a stunning emerald and diamond engagement ring six months ago, saying he was willing to wait a bit longer for the wedding but not the engagement. And now she was here for the party his family was hosting for them.

The door burst open with a flash of red. Rachael in one of her creations. She looked amazing in that above-the-knee style.

"For the love of God, Trisha, people will be here

before you arrive at your own party. Nico sent me up here to root you out, so let's go."

He was waiting at the bottom of the stairs, gorgeous as ever in dark trousers and open-necked white shirt. Casual chic. He grasped her hand while kissing her brow. "You look delicious in that dress, but your neck's a bit bare." He reached into his pocket … Then he was holding up a platinum chain with two entwined hearts encrusted with diamonds, and clasping it at her nape. "Now, let's go to our party."

White lights were sprinkled in the trees and glowing lanterns hung from the balconies and adorned the tables. Clem and Dom managed the BBQs and pizza oven, their clothes covered with white aprons.

When her Canadian cousin, Elise, arrived, Trisha was stunned.

"Oh, my God, how did you get here?"

"Your husband-to-be emailed me, then we talked by phone, and finally he sent his jet for me. How could I resist?"

Trisha grinned. "He's not an easy man to say no to when he sets his mind to something."

Nico sidled up beside her. "Yet you managed it, cara," he said with an arched brow.

"So I did."

"I lived with memories for five years, could never have imagined how fate would throw us back together, so trust me when I say you weren't getting away again."

"Hear, hear," Rachael said with a tilt of her champagne glass. And now I'm going to see what's up with the food."

"And Clem," Nico murmured in Trisha's ear, as she and Elise hugged each other.

"I wish we could see each other more often," she said to Elise, "but for now I'm delighted to have two of my cousins here, and *you* are the most wonderful surprise of the evening."

Dom appeared next to them. "There are a lot of new faces here tonight." He held out his hand to Elise. "I'm Dom, Nico's cousin."

Trisha stepped back. "You go ahead and mix, Elise. We'll catch up."

Nico grasped Trisha's hand as they strolled toward the fire. "Dom didn't waste any time beating a path to Elise. I suspect we'll see your cousins dating mine, which could be interesting."

"It could, except they live in different parts of the world."

"So did we, cara."

"But I was willing to sell Abbott Affairs to Leo and move here."

"Remember, I was also willing to move to Manhattan," he said.

"I know, but thinking of starting a family gave me pause. I didn't want to bring children up in a crowded city."

"The wedding is next week, and then we'll be off on

an extended honeymoon, spending lots of time making those babies. What say you?"

"I say—" she paused, but laughed when she noted his mock frown— *"yes."*

Did you enjoy this book?
If so, you can make a big difference.

Reviews are the most powerful tools I can have when it comes to increasing awareness for my books. Honest reviews help bring them to the attention of many other readers.

If you've enjoyed this book I would be very grateful if you could spend just five minutes leaving a review (it can be as short as you like).

Thanks so much.

You can also sign up for my newsletter with surprise giveaways at http://anncamden.com or find me on Facebook at IndieAuthorAnnCamden.com.

ABOUT THE AUTHOR

Ann Camden writes contemporary romances from her home on Canada's beautiful Atlantic coast. She loves writing about determined heroes and strong heroines who can dish out their share of sassy dialogue. Ann guarantees happy-ever-afters, every time.

Return to Manhattan

When Mia Tremaine's fiancé leaves her without any explanation, it changes the course of her life—and his.

This second-chance romance is a story of fate and the role it plays in their parting, and ultimately what happens when they meet again five years later.

These two people never forgot each other. Which one will take the first step in unearthing the truth needed to mend their lost love?

www.ingramcontent.com/pod-product-compliance
Lightning Source LLC
Chambersburg PA
CBHW022104050726
47591CB00002B/659